LASCIVIOUS SCENES

IN THE

CONVENT

HOW TASSO DILIGENTLY CULTIVATED CERTAIN
WASTE FIELDS, AND MADE OF THEM
A DELIGHTFUL PARADISE

FREELY TRANSLATED FROM THE ITALIAN

BRUXELLES:
PRINTED FOR
SOCIETÉ DES BEAUX ESPRITS
1898

Grove Press, Inc. New York

First Hardcover Edition 1984
First Printing 1984
ISBN: 0-394-53882-X
Library of Congress Catalog Card Number: 83-83190

First Evergreen Edition 1984
First Printing 1984
ISBN: 0-394-62203-0
Library of Congress Catalog Card Number: 83-83190

Printed in the United States of America

GROVE PRESS, INC., 196 West Houston Street,
New York, N.Y., 10014

5 4 3 2 1

INTRODUCTION

Lascivious Scenes in the Convent is one of the most competently and sophisticatedly written volumes of Victorian erotica ever to appear. It would certainly have been deemed a classic in the ranks of *The New Epicurean, Romance of Lust, The Pearl, My Secret Life, Venus in India* and *Memoirs of Dolly Morton,* except for one detail: From the time of its first publication, this book has been almost entirely unknown. It is listed in none of the major bibliographies, and no copy is known to exist in any library open to the public. It is certainly one of the rarest of all volumes of erotica, even more so than *My Secret Life* (of which two sets have been in public collections). The reason for this rarity is itself a product of the Victorian-Edwardian era that saw the first appearance of this novel in 1899. At the turn of the century, popular literature had already come into its own with the advent of cheap methods of printing. The penny magazines hawked on the street corners in the first half of the nineteenth century had given way to popularly priced editions of classic and contemporary works in all genres — all genres, that is, except erotica, which was still seventy years away from such democratic availability. The suppression of sexually explicit literature caused it to be produced in only clandestine, and very limited editions of perhaps a few hundred copies. The costs of such a small print run drove the price of erotica beyond the reach of the general public.

Lascivious Scenes in the Convent was published in an even more restricted fashion than other erotic works of the time. The title page of the book indicates it to be the product of an exclusive organization in Brussels, the "Société des Beaux Esprits." This particular novel was printed in only thirty-five copies. No expense was spared in its production. The edition was deluxe, printed from hand-set type, on large handmade paper, in two colors of ink throughout. It was only by good fortune that a single copy of the work, never before reprinted, was found to exist in a private library, overlooked and lost to the world for decades.

Many readers will recognize its plot as coming from *The Decameron* of Boccaccio, the Italian work first published in the fourteenth century. (The exact story is "Masetto and the Nuns," told in Novel One of Day Three.) *Lascivious Scenes in the Convent* is not simply an English translation of this classic ribald tale. Boccaccio's original was a few short pages, and while free in nature, was delicate in language. Not so this present work. Here is a full-length novel, distinguished by its masterful use of Victorian sexual slang, as well as its explicit descriptions and anti-Romish feelings.

The latter is hardly unique in English literature, or in the works of other European countries. Since the founding of the Church, anti-clerical diatribes and treatises have been common. (One need only to think of Chaucer's fourteenth century *Canterbury Tales*, where the clergy is enjoined to maintain their vows of morality, for if gold — the clergy — were to rust, then what would iron — the common folk — do?) Real or supposed scandals, as well as religious sexual misconduct, have often been the grist of popular pulp reading. Perhaps the most successful of these was the 1836 *Awful Disclosures of Maria Monk*, by the Reverend Slocum. Erotic literatures abound with this anti-clerical theme also. A few examples from the past centuries include: *Thérèse Philosophe* (French, c. 1748, recounting the 1731 scandal involving Father Girard), *Nunnery Tales* (translated from the French c. 1880), *Schwester Monika* (German c. 1815), and *The Adventures of*

Father Silas (English retranslation c. 1890 of the c. 1748 French original). All these used clerical immorality as focus for erotic stimulation. The anti-clerical aspects of this book are used to allow the novices to tell their individual tales of sexual development, initiation, and abuse at the hands of their religious leaders.

—C.J. Scheiner

CONTENTS

CHAPTER I.

WHAT THE NUNS NEEDED

CELIBACY, as it is enjoined in the Roman Church, is not only unwise as being opposed to nature, but it is provocative of the very evils that it is intended to banish and destroy.

Some individuals may have a spiritual gift in that way, but in the greater number of cases, young people, before they understand their nature or themselves, are induced, by reason of their emotional feelings being stirred up and directed by the Church, to take upon themselves vows which, when too late, they find it utterly impossible to carry out.

These emotional feelings are evanescent in their character, and are easily overpowered, either by the strong natural instinct of propagation, which becomes developed in most people as they grow to maturity, or when they are brought into contact with temptations of a lascivious tendency. And these very temptations, strange to say, they are sure to meet with sooner or later in the confessional.

There are abundant historical proofs of the truth of these statements in every country where that form of religion has prevailed; and nowhere more than in Italy, its great centre, and also among the ecclesiastics and religious bodies which there abound.

The following story, the facts of which are well authenticated, affords an interesting and amusing illustration.

There was, in the suburbs of a northern city, a handsome building, with well-kept gardens and grounds. This house was occupied by a sisterhood of nuns under the care of a Mother Abbess. She was a titled lady by birth, and in her younger days had been married to an old man. She was naturally of a voluptuous disposition, and not being satisfied by her husband, consoled herself in the arms of a young noble of their acquaintance. On one occasion they were surprised in the very act by her husband. The aged man made a furious onslaught on her gallant. In defending himself the younger man unfortunately ran him through with his rapier. The affair caused much scandal, and she, to make the best amend she could, took the veil, and retired into a convent. She had a brother, a Bishop; and by his influence and her own energy and talents, she was gradually promoted, until now, in her thirty-fifth year, she was made a Mother Abbess. She had under her charge twenty-four nuns, chiefly of her own selection. They were all good-looking young women, with the exception of four, who, being elderly, were chosen as examples of sanctity and strict adherance to convent rules and discipline.

The grounds and gardens were kept in order by an old man who slept outside the Convent bounds. He had managed to scrape together a little money, and at the time of our story felt that his years unfitted him for his work; and so he resolved to resign his post, and pass the remainder of his days in quiet and ease.

The position was a good and lucrative one, and was sought after by many. Among others was a nephew of the old gardener's named Tasso, who wished to obtain it. He possessed good qualifications for the post, as he had been trained on the property of a nobleman in the South, but he was a comparative stranger in the district in which the Convent was situated. He requested his uncle to recommend him, but the old man assured him that it would be of no use, for the objection would be that he was young, well-made, and altogether too good-looking; and he knew that the Mother Abbess, who prided herself on the reputation for sanctity which the Convent had acquired, would in all probability decline to engage anyone but a man, tolerably old, and not so prepossessing in appearance.

"And she is right," he added, "for among the holy Sisters are some young women that seem to me to be ready for almost any sort of mischief, — and from the way I have seen them sporting with one another, when they thought they were unobserved, I think that under their sober vestal garb they have as skittish natures as any girls I have ever seen."

This only made young Tasso all the more eager; for, like the war horse, he smelled the battle from afar, and his blood warmed for the fray.

"Well, uncle," he replied. "Don't oppose me. Give me your consent, and let me endeavor by my own wits to induce the Mother Abbess to give me at least a fair trial."

Now Tasso was not only a young man of enterprise, but he was also singularly intelligent and wise in his generation. With great craft he determined to represent himself as being deaf and dumb, and to assume a heavy and stolid appearance. By what arts he persuaded his uncle to give him the desired recommendation, and by what means he obtained the old man's promise of secrecy, history does not tell us. We only know that when he went to the Mother Abbess with a note of introduction from his uncle, he had artfully disguised as much as possible his good looks and youthful appearance, and he communicated with her by means of a slate which he carried with him, and on which she wrote her questions to him and he replied in fairly legible writing.

She was pleased with the recommendations he had, and pitied his infirmities, but was rather repelled by his uncouth manner and unkempt hair; but on considering the matter she thought that after all, his not being very inviting in appearance, and especially his being deaf and dumb, might be of great advantage, as it would certainly render him less communicative either inside or outside the Convent.

So she finally engaged him on a month's trial.

Upon the following day Tasso entered on his duties. He knew his business well, and apparently thought of nothing else.

Now it was the custom of the Sisters to take exercise at certain hours in the Convent grounds. They looked at him in a friendly way, and some of them made bold to speak a few kind words. But to these advances he would always reply by a shake of his head, at the same time pointing to his ears and lips. Then he would hold out his slate, — which, when not in use, he carried in his pocket, — for them to write any commands they wished to give. But the Mother Abbess, ever on the watch, soon saw that he made no attempt to communicate with them of his own accord; and convinced that this was the right man for the place at last, and relying on his simplicity, she relaxed her vigilance, and gave her attention to more pressing duties.

After a while, the Sisters realized that he was deaf and dumb, and seemed to forget his presence, talking to one another just as if he was not there at all.

They thought him stupid as well as deaf, but all the while he kept his eyes open and his ears attentive, so that nothing passed unnoticed that came within their reach. Soon he had learned the names of all the Sisters, and could recognize them by their voices.

Two of the younger nuns, Lucia and Robina, seemed to have taken a fancy to him, for they often walked near where he was at work, and always gave him a smile as they passed.

There were many rustic seats scattered about, in shady spots, and these were much used by the nuns in their hours of recreation.

Whenever Tasso was occupied near any of these seats, the Sisters Lucia and Robina were sure to come and sit there and watch him, while they talked or worked at their embroidery.

Their usual conversation was of convent

matters, such as their work or their teaching, —for nearly all the nuns took part in the instruction of the young ladies who attended the Convent School.

But on one occasion they commenced to talk of their Confessors. Lucia declared that she liked Father Joachim best, for he seemed to take more interest in the Convent.

"Only," she added, "He does ask such bothering questions."

"What kind of questions?" asked Robina, with a smile.

"Why, Sister! Don't you know we're not allowed to tell anything outside the confessional of what takes place within? However, you and I are such friends that we may disregard these hard rules when we are talking confidentially together, — may we not?"

"Yes, certainly. Go on."

Here Tasso, who appeared to be very busy, moved a little nearer, and worked noiselessly.

"Well, the other night I had a queer dream. I had been looking, during the day, at a fine picture of St. Martin, painted by Titian; and when I was asleep, I thought that I saw him coming towards me with no clothing on at all, and Oh! he looked so very beautiful. As he advanced, I saw something between his legs, though I cannot tell you what it was like. But while I was looking at it, he came up and lay down over me. And I thought I felt his body pressing mine in a most delightful way, and I got a delicious feeling in the corresponding part of myself. Then I suddenly awoke, and — what do you think? I had one of my fingers pushed right up into myself, and I could not stop rubbing it in and out until I became all wet. Since then I have put my hand there several times, and it always gives me great pleasure. Now, of course, I know this is all very wrong, and I had to confess it to the priest."

"And what were his bothering questions?"

"Oh! He made me describe exactly where my finger was. I had to tell him, it was in my woman's slit, between the soft lips that we have there. Then he asked what was it I saw between St. Martin's legs, and if I knew what it was for? I felt annoyed at such a question, and said, 'How could I tell? I suppose it was what all men have there.'

"Then he asked, for these holy Fathers never seem to feel abashed, if I ever thought about a man's part, and whether I had any longing to see it, and know what it was like?

"I confessed that I had felt some curiosity about it, but that I always tried to banish such thoughts from my mind.

"He said that it was quite right, that such thoughts were natural to both men and women, and all that was required was not to allow them to dwell in the mind. Then he told me to come to him soon again, and tell him all my thoughts, and that he would hear my confession in the Mother Abbess' private room. Since then I have been thinking more than ever about these very things; and do you know, Robina, I have quite a longing to know what a man's thing is like? Haven't you?"

"Sometimes, dear. But it is very likely that Father Joachim may gratify your longing himself. I fancy he has some such intention in his mind, and that's why he said he would hear your confession in the Mother Abbess' private room. Meantime, let me tell you that these lusty priests use the confessional as a means of gratifying their own sensual desires. They know that we poor nuns are quite in their power, and they dearly love to make us tell them every secret thought which naturally comes into our minds as women, with regard to the other sex. And more than that, they often suggest the thoughts themselves, and when we are at a loss, they supply the words too. It does seem strange to me, if these things are as wicked as they declare in their public teaching, why they encourage them so directly in their secret ministrations in the confessonal. Now I'll tell you, Lucia, what I shall propose: Let us be true to one another; and consult together to get all the fun we can out of these holy Fathers, and at the same time enjoy any little pleasure that comes in our way, for indeed ours is a hard lot."

"I quite agree with you, dear Robina," said Lucia, "and gladly accept your proposal, for I too am heartily sick of the tiresome round of these vigils, fasts, prayers and penances, which instead of making us better, only drive us to something worse, as a mere matter of relief. We never see any thing in the shape of a man, except these oily priests, with their sensual mouths and wicked-looking eyes. Somehow I don't trust them, and I can't abide them. Now there is some comfort in looking at this poor, honest, hard-working fellow,

Tasso. And, Robina, have you noticed how well made he is? Look at his nicely-turned limbs!"

"You are right, Lucia," replied Robina. "There is some satisfaction in looking at him. And indeed I was just thinking that, if we could see him as you saw St. Martin in your dream, we should behold a very satisfactory illustration of that special part which is most interesting to us as women. Is that what you were thinking of, you rogue?"

And looking at her with glittering eyes, she gave her a nudge with her elbow.

Lucia laughed merrily.

"Why not, my dear? Father Joachim says that such thoughts are only natural; and as we are forever shut off from the reality, it cannot be so very wrong for us to console ourselves with the thought."

"Quite so," replied Robina. "But let me tell you a notion which has come into my head, I don't know how. May we not try at least to turn our thought into reality? Could we not manage to induce Tasso in some way to gratify our curiosity? He is so simple that I am sure he would think nothing of showing all he has to us, if we could but make him feel that we would neither be frightened nor affronted, nor tell anyone. Now what do you think of that notion, Lucia?"

"Capital, dear! But how can it be brought about?"

"I'll tell you one way that we might obtain our object, even without his knowledge. I noticed yesterday when one of the Sisters brought him a glass of our light wine as a reward for moving her rose-trees so nicely, that after he drank it, he stole away among the laurels near our Little-house, (a name they had for a place of convenience in a corner of the grounds,) and I fancy he went there to make water. Now it occurs to me that if one of us got him some drink this hot day, and the other went to hide in the Little-house, she would have a chance of getting a view of that part of him which we would both like to see, and then she could tell the other all that occurred."

"You are very clever, Sister Robina," replied Lucia, "and you know many things of which I am ignorant. I cordially approve of your plan, and if you will place yourself in ambush in the Little-house, I will run for the drink. — But mind! You must describe to me afterwards everything you have seen, with the greatest precision."

"All right! Let us go away together, and I will steal round to the hiding-place without his seeing me."

Tasso fairly grinned with delight. His crafty device was already bearing fruit, and his manly organ bounded with exultation at the thought of anticipated triumph.

Lucia quickly reappeared with a cup brimming with love-inspiring drink. He took it from her hands with a grateful nod, and immediately drank it off. On receiving the cup again, she turned away to bring it back to the house. Tasso at once made off to the corner indicated, and having placed himself in full view before the door, which was pierced with holes for the purpose of ventilation, he took out his middle limb, and exhibited its full length and even the large appendages beneath. It was a splendid specimen of a fresh-colored prick, large and strong, in the full flush of youthful power and beauty. Holding it in his hand, he made his water shoot out before him in a way that could not fail to be most interesting to a female observer. Then he drew down the soft white skin so as to uncover all the glowing head, now of a bright rosy tint. He shook it from side to side until the last amber drop had fallen, and then, as if yielding to some sudden impulse, he began to imitate the common fucking motion by vigorously working his posteriors and making his prick pass swiftly backwards and forwards through his hands.

The hidden watcher eyes it with the same regard a famished wolf has for a tempting morsel. Her bosoms heave and swell like the ocean billows scurrying before the storm. In vain she grasps them with her hands. In vain she tries to calm the rapid tumultuous beating of her heart. Her breath comes quickly. It is frequently interrupted by the soft sighs which escape her. Something within her seems to jump, and then a flame devours her. Instinctively one hand strays from throbbing bosom down to her robe. The black garb is quickly drawn up, and her hand touches the mossy charms beneath. Passion's hottest fires are already flaming furiously. Yonder, in the thicket, is the only solace that will afford her relief. Ah! If she only had it in her grasp! A rosy mist floats before her eyes. In its very midst, surrounded by a

golden halo, she sees the gardener's own tool,
— the glorious badge of manhood that Tasso
alone possesses. Its ruby head turns toward
her. Look! It quivers with passion. A few
pearly drops ooze from it, glitter in the sun-
light, and fall. Then the vision fades from
her view.

For, with a faint sigh of satisfaction, Tasso
has pushed it in under cover again, and
has buttoned up his trowsers. And the crunch
of gravel under his feet a moment later informs
the passionate girl that Tasso is returning to
his work.

CHAPTER II.

HOW THEY OBTAINED IT

T ASSO'S great hope was that the two Sisters would return to their seat, and favor him a little more by their delightful conversation. Nor was he disappointed. The Sisters quickly reappeared, and bringing with them their embroidery, sat down in the seat they had occupied before.

Tasso was conscious that they now regarded him with peculiar interest, and that their eyes looked as if they were trying to penetrate that portion of his attire. He therefore pushed it out and made it prominent as much as he could.

Lucia was speaking.

"Well, Robina, you certainly had a grand

success. How I envy you! It must have been delightful to watch him, when he thought he was all alone, first piddling and then actually playing with his thing! But now, tell me, like a good dear, exactly what it was like: its size, its color, and above all, tell me its shape."

"You must try and see it yourself, my dear," replied Robina, "for it is not an easy thing to describe. It seemed about eight inches long, and nearly as thick as your wrist, but quite round. It is covered with a soft white skin which slips easily up and down. When he pulled this skin back, the top stood up like a large round head, shelving to a point, and of a purplish red color. It was that which attracted me most, and, my dear, it had a most wonderful effect on myself. My hairy slit began to thrill and to throb in such a way that, for the life of me, I could not help pulling up my dress and rubbing it with my hand. And it grew hotter and hotter, until a warm flow came, and gave me relief."

"What a delightful time you must have had, Robina," commented Lucia. "Do you know your telling me all this has made mine frightfully hot, too?" And she twisted about,

rubbing her bottom on the seat. "How I wish
Tasso was not watching us. I would ask you
to put your kind hand on my slit and afford
me a little of the same pleasure."

Robina laughed.

"I fancy he's not thinking of us at all. He
is too dull to have any notions of that kind.
Stand up, dear, as if you were pulling some
buds from the branch overhanging us, and I
will slip my hand up from behind, so that he
can see nothing. Now, do you like that,
dear?"

"Oh! Your fingers are giving me great
pleasure!" replied the excited Lucia. "There!
That's the place!—Push it up!—Oh!
Wouldn't it be nice to have Tasso's delightful
thing poking me there!—You said, Robina,
that was Nature's intention, and that the
mutual touch of our differently formed parts
gives the greatest satisfaction. What fools
we were to give it up!"

"What a child you are, Lucia! The holy
Fathers will teach you that you may enjoy it
now more than ever, and without doing
anything wrong, either, only it must be done
with them alone."

"Now! Oh! Now, Robina!—Push your

finger up! As far as you can! How I long for Tasso's dear thing! — Oh! Oh! — That will do!"

And she sat down, and leaned her head against Robina for support.

It will be easily understood what an over-powering effect this scene had on poor Tasso. His sturdy prick, glowing with youthful vigor, seemed to be trying to break its covering and burst into open view.

The unsuspecting talk of the two Sisters almost maddened him. He felt that if he could only present his "dear thing," as they called it, openly before them, he might obtain from one or the other, or from perhaps both, the sweet favor he desired.

In this mood he gradually worked up close to them, and slyly unbuttoned his clothes down the front.

He restrained himself, however, for the present, that he might learn something more from the Sisters, who went on talking.

"But Robina, what shall we do about confessing this touching of ourselves and one another to the priests? If we conceal it, our confession is incomplete and sinful, as they tell us we ought to make a full avowal of all our faults and shortcomings. You know how they are always urging this upon us as a sacred duty. And if we give him the slightest hint, Father Joachim will be sure to worm out from us all about Tasso, and that might do him much harm, and cause him to be sent away, — and we too may be separated, and not allowed to walk with one another."

"Quite true, Lucia. We must do all we can to guard against these two evils. And there really is no way but to keep the whole matter a secret between ourselves. I, for my part, won't let that press upon my conscience, as I now know that there is so much humbug and deceit about the confessional that I have no faith in it as a religious duty at all."

"I am with you again, Robina," replied Lucia. "It would be an awful wrong to injure poor Tasso, who is quite innocent; and if you and I were separated, — why, I should die, and that would be the end of it."

Tasso was greatly pleased at hearing this, for his mind was now satisfied that so far as these two Sisters were concerned, he had no cause to dread exposure and its certain consequences.

"Well, Lucia, dear, we'll try to prevent

that, at all events. We shall have to go to the priest, but we must carefully avoid all reference to anyone but ourselves. It will be great fun, I am sure, to confess our looking at and petting our own slits. We can tell him our dreams also. That will sufficiently please him, and perhaps draw him on to commit himself with us, and then he will have to keep quiet for his own sake."

And they both laughed at the thought.

Just then, a little accident happened to Tasso which gave a sudden turn to their conversation. As he was bending at his work, his foot slipped, and he rolled over on his back. This motion, in the most natural way, set his prick free, and it started out, looking very stiff and inflamed.

He quickly jumped up, and looking at his naked prick with stupid amazement, began to utter uncouth sounds, like an ordinary donkey: "Hoo! Awe!" And he made some ineffectual attempts to push it back into its place.

"There! Lucia," cried Robina. "Your wish is granted. This poor simple fellow has accidentally given you the view for which you were longing. Don't you admire it?"

"Yes!— But what should we do, Robina, if

any of the Sisters were to come up now?
What a hubbub there would be! — But see!
— I declare, he can't get it back."

"Well, go and help him, Lucia. Make
haste, and I will keep a lookout."

Lucia's eyes were intently fastened on the
interesting object. Her face was flushed, and
she looked altogether extremely excited. She
had no time however, for reflection. So she
jumped up, as her friend advised, went to
Tasso, and tried to help to get his rebellious
tool back into its hiding-place.

Taking advantage of his apparent simplicity,
and wishing to expedite matters, she took hold
of his prick with her hand.

But Oh! How the touch of that piece of
animated flesh thrilled her! It felt so warm
and soft, yet so firm and strong! She could
neither bend it, nor push it back. And the
more she made the effort, the more strongly
did it resist and stand out.

"Oh! dear! Oh! dear! What shall I do,
Robina? It won't go back for me!"

Robina laughed until the tears ran down her
cheeks.

"Anyway, take him along," she replied.
" Bring him into the summer-house."

This happened to be conveniently near, and was well screened by bushes. Lucia with a smile, pointed it out to Tasso, and still holding his prick, gently drew him on.

Tasso, putting on a most innocent look, went readily with her, and Robina followed in the rear.

As they entered the leafy shade, she said: "Now, Lucia, you have him all to yourself. If you don't succeed in getting him to do every thing you want, you are a less clever girl than I take you to be. If all else fails, just show him your mossy nest, and that will draw him as surely as a magnet attacts a piece of iron. Meantime I'll keep a sharp lookout here at the door."

But, in very truth, Tasso did not need much drawing. His prick was throbbing with desire. It was fairly burning to get into the folds of her soft recess. Yet he checked himself, in order to see what she would do.

She led him on until she backed against the inner seat. Then she sat down, and he remained standing before her. In this position his prick was now close to her face. She rubbed it softly between her hands, and then kissed its glowing head. She moved it over her nose and cheeks, sniffing up with delight the peculiar odor which exhaled from it.

Every time she brought it to her lips, Tasso pushed it gently against her mouth. Her lips gradually opened, and the prick seemed to pop in of its own accord. He felt her pliant tongue playing over its head, and twining round its indented neck. The sensation was so delicious that he could not help uttering a deep guttural "Ugh!" and pressing up against her.

She yielded to his pressure, and very soon he had her reclining on her back flat on the seat. Then bending over her he quickly drew up her nun's robes, and lifting her legs he pressed her thighs down on her body in such a way as to expose the whole of her beautiful bottom, and give him a full view of her delicious love chink, surrounded with luxuriant hair. Oh! How it seemed to pout out with a most unspeakable delight! He took his prick in his hand, and rubbed its glowing head between the soft moist lips.

This action proved just as pleasant to her as it was delightful to him. She pushed upwards to meet him, and called to her friend:

"Look! Robina! There has been no failure,

— he's just a-going to do it. Pity you could not come and watch it going in! Oh! It does feel nice! — Oh! So nice!"

"Ha! Ha! My dear," laughed Robina, "you will have to suffer a little before you know how really nice it is!"

Tasso now began to push in good earnest, and Lucia winced not a little as she felt the sharp pain, caused by the head of his huge prick forcing its way through the tight embrace of her vagina, for she was a true virgin, and her hymen had never been ruptured. However, she bore it bravely, especially as she knew her friend was watching.

"Robina," she called, to show her indifference to the pain, " I wish you would go behind and give him a shove, to make him push harder."

But just as she spoke, the obstructing hymen suddenly gave way, and his fine prick rushed up and filled all the inside of her cunt, and his hard balls flapped up against her bottom.

"Ah!" she cried, as she felt the inward rush of the vigorous tool. "Now it's all over! He's got it all in! — Well, it wasn't so bad after all. And now it feels delicious! — How nicely he makes it move in and out. — Can you see it, Robina?" she asked, as she noticed her friend stooping behind Tasso, and looking up between his legs.

"Yes, dear Lucia. I see your pretty slit sucking in his big tool, and I feel his two balls gathered up tightly in their bag. He certainly is no fool at this kind of work. I am sure he is just going to spurt his seed into you. — There! — Tell me, do you like it?"

"Oh! Yes! It feels grand! — He's shedding such a lot into me! And more is coming, too! It is the nicest thing I have ever felt!"

And throwing her arms about him she hugged him with all her might.

Presently he drew his prick out of her warm sheath. It was slightly tinged with blood, — the token of his victory and her pain. Robina carefully wiped it with her handkerchief, and coaxed him to sit down between them on the seat. Then they made signs to him to produce his slate.

Lucia wrote:

"Dear Tasso. I greatly enjoyed what you did to me. Have you any name for it, that I may know what to ask for when I want it again?"

He smiled when he read the question, and then wrote a reply.

"It is called fucking."

Then he handed her the slate.

"Doing this is called fucking," she said to Robina.

Then pointing to his prick, which was beginning to stand again, in all the pride of youthful vigor, she wrote:

"What is the name of this?"

"It is called a 'prick' and yours is a 'cunt'," he wrote, "and they are made for one another."

Lucia laughed when she read it.

"Why, Robina," she cried, "we are getting a grand lesson. His thing is a prick and our slits are cunts; but he need not have told us that they are made for one another, for all the world knows that. What a pity he can't talk! I would so much like to hear him speak of his prick and our cunts. But it is well that he can write about them."

Then she took the slate and wrote:

"Your prick is getting quite large and stiff again. Would you like to fuck Sister Robina?"

Tasso grinned.

"Do you know what I have just written?" said Lucia, turning to Robina. "I have asked him if he would like to fuck you?"

"Oh! You horrid girl!" retorted Robina.

"Of course he will say he would. Men always love a change of cunts. I suppose we must use that word now when talking to each other."

Tasso's delight was almost insupportable. He longed to use his tongue, and give audible expression to his joy. But that would have spoiled everything. So he resolved to persevere with his role, and wrote:

"If Sister Robina will follow your kind example, and grant me the same favor, it will call forth the everlasting gratitude of poor dumb Tasso."

"Why, he has written quite a nice little speech, Robina," said Lucia, handing her the slate.

" He writes a fairly good hand, too," smilingly remarked Robina; and then handing back the slate, said, " Tell him to stand up, and let me kiss his prick as you did."

Lucia wrote accordingly:

"Stand up, Tasso, and let her kiss your prick first, and then you can fuck her cunt just as much as you like."

Tasso at once complied. He stood before Robina, and pushed between her knees so as to place his prick more conveniently for her eager inspection and caresses.

Taking it tenderly in her hands, she felt it all over, as if measuring its size and power to give pleasure. Then she turned her attention to the heavy bags which held his large stones, and pushed her fingers back even as far as the aperture behind.

Tasso repaid the caresses she gave him by bending to one side, and thrusting his hand up between her warm thighs. He grasped the fat lips of her cunt, and rubbed the hot clitoris which jutted out between them. Then, as they both became eager for the sweet consummation to which these thrilling touches led, he gently pushed her back. She yielded readily enough, for her cunt was already moist with the expectation of taking in the delicious morsel she held in her hands. She allowed him to uncover all her hidden charms, and spread her thighs to their utmost extent. But just as she felt him inserting his fiery tool, she called to Lucia, who, though standing at the door, was intently watching Tasso s interesting operation.

"Dear Lucia, keep a strict watch! It would be an awful thing if anyone caught us here!"

"Don't be afraid," replied Lucia. "I'll keep

a good lookout. There's no one about now, and I only take a peep now and then to see how you and Tasso are enjoying yourselves. I love to watch you. I was just thinking, that next to being fucked one's self, there is nothing like watching another going through it. I never saw your cunt look so well as it did just now, when Tasso opened the lips, and rubbed the head of his prick inside the rosy folds. And now he has got it all in. It is most delightful to watch it slipping in and out. But how is it that he does not seem to hurt you as he did me? For I notice that he got in quite easily, and you kept hugging him closely all the time! — Oh! How nice it must have felt!"

And Lucia pressed her hands between her own legs, and jerked her bottom backwards and forwards.

"My! How you talk, Lucia! But anyway, keep a good lookout, and you may watch me between times. I don't mind your seeing how much we are enjoying ourselves. Poor Tasso can't hear me, or I would tell him how well pleased I am. I am sure the squeezing of my cunt is making him feel that already."

She breathes heavily, and heaves her bottom up convulsively to meet his rapid thrusts.

"You might put your hand on us now, Lucia, if you like. — He's just finishing. — Oh! It's grand!"

And all her muscles relaxed as she reclined back, and Tasso lay panting on her belly.

Lucia sat down by them, and leaned over Tasso, squeezing her thighs together, for she felt her own fount of pleasure in the flow.

After a moment's rest, Tasso got up, shook himself, and having arranged his clothes, wrote on his slate:

"Dear kind ladies: You have made poor dumb Tasso very happy. Let me now thank you and return to my work, lest any harm should happen."

He then bowed himself out, and disappeared among the laurels.

CHAPTER III.

HOW ROBINA ENJOYED IT

O N THE following day, to Tasso's great delight, the two young nuns again sat near him, though in a different part of the grounds.

The sight of him naturally made them think of their late pleasures, and they began to talk of how and when they might safely meet him again in the summer-house.

Having been now fairly launched on the sea of pleasure, they felt irresistibly impelled to go on. They knew that they were running a tremendous risk, but the temptation was so great that they were ready to brave all the consequences.

So, watching their opportunity, they told Tasso on his slate that, if possible, they would come out that evening during the half hour allowed the nuns for private devotion before the usual service. It was his time for quitting work, putting away his tools, and retiring for the night, and the garden was then generally empty.

Lucia then reminded her friend that she had promised to tell her how it was that she felt no smart or pain when Tasso pushed his prick into her cunt.

"My dear Lucia," began Robina, "I think I may tell you, now that we understand one another, and have shaken off our terror of the confessional. Before I came here, I had for my Confessor a priest with a great appearance of sanctity; but, as I found to my cost, it was only a cloak to hide his real nature. He was of a strong lustful temperament. Why, dear, he actually forced me in the room of the Mother Superior, where he heard my confession. I often think he had me there with an evil design which the Superior not only had connived at, but helped to carry out. And strange to say, my confessions furnished him with the occasion he desired.

"I had to confess what arose out of a curious

circumstance, — something like your dream. It happened thus:

"The evening before making my first confession after joining the Sisterhood of M——, I obtained permission to take a solitary walk of meditation in a field belonging to the Convent. Feeling tired, I sat down by the boundary hedge to rest. I had my Manual with me, and oddly enough was reading that part of the preparation for confession where the sins against chastity are referred to, and we are directed to examine our own conscience, and are asked if we have looked at indecent pictures, or touched either ourselves or others immodestly, etc., when I heard the voices of a a man and a woman on the other side of the hedge.

"As they come up, the man said: 'See! What a fine sheltered spot! — Just what we were looking for!'

"Then they sat down and settled themselves on the grass. From their talk, they must have at once commenced playing with each other's private parts. They used such terms as 'prick,' and 'cunt,' and 'fucking,' which were then new to me. But I was at no loss to understand their meaning, from their talk, and the manner in which the words were applied.

"The man said: 'Pull up your petticoats as as high as you can, and open your legs, so as to give me a full view of your pretty brown-haired cunt! — That's a dear! — Oh! How luscious it looks! So hot and so moist! So velvety inside!'

"'I am glad you like it!' she replied. 'But don't keep it waiting too long! Put in your prick and fuck me!'

"I know it was a very wicked thing to do, to remain there, listening to all this, but my curiosity was so great that I could not tear myself away.

"I then heard sounds, as if they were struggling or working together, and then she spoke in a gasping voice.

"Oh! I feel it up — ever so far!' she said. 'Push! My darling! — Push!'

"And then I heard their bellies smack together.

"'Oh! Oh!' she cried. 'Your dear prick is filling my cunt with the most unspeakable delight!'

"He panted loudly as she continued. 'Oh! My love! That is so nice!'

"I listened to this with breathless interest, and the effect upon myself was overpowering. Without thinking of what I was doing, I put my hand on my affair, and rubbed it until I obtained relief. And while I was so occupied, they departed.

"This touching and rubbing I later confessed to the priest, and then I had to tell him the occasion and the circumstances, and had to repeat every word which I heard used. But I objected to saying such names, on the score of decency. To this he replied that there was no such a thing as indecency in the confessional, for it was a holy place, and it imparted a holy character to everything that was said and done at that time. So he made me say 'prick,' over and over again, and then asked me what I supposed it was.

"I replied that it seemed to me to be the name for the private part of a man, and that the other word I had heard, 'cunt,' was the corresponding part of the woman, and that 'fucking' was the joining of them together, which Nature made us understand was a very pleasant thing.

"Then he made me describe the excitement I felt in my own cunt during the time I was engaged in listening to the man and woman who were fucking.

"And as if this were not enough, he told me he wanted to know exactly how I put my hand on my cunt, and to let him see me do it.

"This, however, I at first flatly refused to do. My obstinacy angered him; for his face, which had been very red before, now grew purple, and his eyes looked as if they were starting out of his head.

"He caught me roughly by the arm. — I was kneeling by his side, you know. — He shook me as he said :

" 'Daughter, you have not yet learned the first of all virtues, — obedience.   Stand up!'

"I did so.

"Now lift up your skirts and place your hand just as you have been describing it to me !'

"I jerked out the word 'Never!' through my compressed lips.

"He arose from the chair in which he had been sitting, and pushed me violently towards a sofa at the side of the room. He forced me down upon this, and then began pulling up my clothes.

" 'How dare you!' I said, in a very angry voice. 'If you were ten times a priest, I would not suffer you to take such liberties with me! Let me up, or I will cry out!'

"At this very moment, the Mother Superior walked in and came up, looking exceedingly vexed.

" 'Sister Robina! How can you behave in this unseemly manner? I am very sorry to find that I have such a refractory nun under my charge. Don't you know that you must obey this holy Father in all things?'

" 'But I won't obey him,' I retorted, 'when he wants me to do something that I believe to be wrong.'

" 'There you make a mistake,' was her reply. 'You may be sure that what a priest in the confessional requires you to do is always necessary and right. And even though the thought may be disagreeable to you, yet you are bound to submit.'

" 'I won't!' I declared.

" 'You shall!' she retorted, catching me by the shoulders, and pushing me over.

" I struggled with her, while the priest at the same time held my legs with one of his strong hands, and pulled up my clothes with the other.

"Between them both, I was powerless, and began to cry as I said:

" 'You are making me break my vows!'

" 'Not in the least, you silly girl. Don't you know he is under a vow as well as you are? And two vows, like two negatives, nullify one another. You are each only prevented from going with others, and your submission will be a praise-worthy act, for it will afford both him and yourself a necessary relief. Come, now! Show us that you understand the matter aright. Open your thighs, and let him see all that you have there. Nature meant that to be used, and in this manner; and with my sanction you can do so without blame. I heard what you just confessed, and approve of your using all those terms when engaged here with the holy Father.'

"But her fine sophistry did not quiet me. I still opposed them in every way I could.

"By this time the priest had forcibly drawn up my skirts, and all my thighs, belly and bottom were exposed before him. He had even lifted my legs as well, and as I kicked them in the air in my struggles to get free, he pinched my naked bottom in the most savage manner, maddening me with pain, and making me jerk about in a manner that added greatly to his delight. I saw that his eyes were fixed upon my cunt, which I felt opening at every bound. He kept my legs wide apart, but I still struggled so hard that he was not able to place his hands upon my slit.

"Vexed at what she termed my silly obstinacy, the Mother Superior reprimanded me severely.

" 'You stupid thing!' she exclaimed. 'Keep quiet. Let him look at that saucy impudent cunt of yours. He shall do any thing with it that he likes! — Now, Father Angelo, take your prick and thrust it well in! — It will be a good punishment, and only serve her right. — But show it to her first, that she may get the full benefit of the sight before she feels your hard firm thrusts.'

"He at once complied; and, taking out his prick, he stood up close to me. It was the first man's prick I had ever seen, and it terrified me by its extreme length, and its huge red head. All at once, he pushed it towards my face.

" 'Oh ! Fie !' I cried. 'Take the monstrous thing away. — It is horrible !'

" And I shut my eyes.

" But the Mother Superior and the priest only laughed at me.

" 'What a fool you are !' she exclaimed.

" And taking the prick in her hand, she rubbed it over my face, made it pass under my nose, and about my mouth. In vain I tried to turn from it. She always managed to keep the firm warm thing playing around my face, until it nearly set me wild. And yet not altogether with anger, for strange to say, though I certainly disliked the man, still the touch of his prick and its peculiar smell had an effect on me which I could not resist. I began to feel a kind of pleasure in having my cunt exposed to his view, and felt a thrill of delight run through my veins when he put his hand on my slit and caressed the lips and tickled the clitoris.

" Noticing this, the Mother Superior removed the charger, and addressing the priest, said:

" 'Now, Father, you may try her. She seems tired out, or perhaps, — and I hope it is so, — she is coming to a better mind.'

"Then she put her hand softly under my chin, turned up my mouth and kissed me.

" 'Come, Sister,' she said. 'Take my advice. Submit gracefully, and it will be all the better for you. Know then, that I am fully resolved that you shall not leave this room until you have been well fucked.'

"Father Angelo then drew me to the end of the sofa, until my bottom rested on the very edge. He then fixed himself between my thighs, and spreading open the lips of my cunt with his fingers, while he pressed the head of his big red tool firmly against the entrance.

"Madame knelt on the floor beside us, and tucking up my clothes as high as she could, watched the operation.

"He pushed gently at first, then harder and harder, and hurt me considerably. I moaned with the pain, but I did not resist, for I now saw it was of no use, and I began to be on fire, and wish his tool was safely lodged inside.

"The Mother Superior now leaned over me and opening my bodice, drew up my breasts, and caressed the exposed bubbies with her hand.

"Then turning to him, she said, 'Can't you get in? Is it too tight? — Just wet her cunt and your prick, and you will find it easier.'

"He took away his prick, and in a moment I felt his tongue moving around the inside of my cunt, and his lips sucking my clitoris.

"This had a strangely soothing and most delightful effect, and I smiled with pleasure.

" 'Ah! — You like that!' she said. 'You like to have your cunt licked and your clitoris sucked, do you? Well, you won't have the full pleasure until he gets his prick in, and drives it all the way up.'

"Meanwhile the priest was moistening his prick with spittle, and again placed it between the lips of my anxious slit. This time I did not shrink from his attack at all, but spread my thighs as widely apart as I could.

" 'Now, Father, push,' she cried; and putting her hand down, she grasped and squeezed my clitoris.

"I could feel the great hard head forcing its way in. You know now, Lucia, what a strange sensation of mingled pain and pleasure a woman experiences the first time a man's prick is driven into her cunt—"

"Shall I ever forget?" responded Lucia, with animation. "But in my case, the pain was only for a moment, for soon it was completely overbalanced by the pleasure."

"Yes; so I was glad to see," responded Robina. "But Tasso's prick in not by any means as thick as that of Father Angelo."

Poor Tasso's jaw fell a little as he listened to this confession.

"And somehow," she continued, "he uses his in a more gentle and coaxing way."

"So he does!" assented Lucia. "And Oh! Robina! I am longing so for it now. — But go on. Tell me how they finished the job, and how you liked it."

"Well," resumed Robina, " the touch of Madame's fingers excited me greatly, and I met the next push he gave with an upward heave. I at once felt something give way inside, and the hot stiff prick glided up into my cunt and filled the whole cavity with such a sensation of voluptuous delight as I had never experienced before in my life. The Mother Superior kissed me again; and she squeezed the lips of my cunt around his prick as she asked me this question:

" 'Now, Robina, how do you like that? — Could there be any thing nicer than the feel of a man's prick stirring that way in your cunt? May he fuck you when he wishes hereafter?'

" 'Oh! Oh! It's delicious! — Yes! He may fuck me as much as he likes,' I could not help adding, as I felt the great prick moving swiftly in and out. 'Oh! Oh! That is so — so — nice!'

"Madame seemed well pleased at her success. Nothing gave her so much pleasure, I afterwards learned, as seeing a woman fucked for the first time; and in the pursuit of this form of pleasure, she had had every one of her nuns fucked by one or another of the priests who acted as Confessors."

"I am sure," said Lucia, "that it is very pleasant to stand by and watch another woman being fucked. I know I liked to look at you while Tasso was fucking you. I dearly love to watch a prick working in and out between the hairy lips of your cunt. But go on, — tell me more."

"The Mother Superior asked me," Robina

continued, "if I enjoyed the feel of her hand about my cunt while it was being fucked.

" 'It greatly increases the pleasure,' I replied.

" 'I expected it would,' she said. 'And now let me put your hands on mine, and perhaps that will not only add still more to your enjoyment, but also give me a little taste of the pleasure, as well.'

"Speaking thus, she drew up her clothes, and placed my hand between her thighs. I pushed it up until I met an immense pair of thick hairy lips, and, diving my fingers into the chink between I felt a cunt overflowing with moisture, and burning with heat.

"I rubbed my hand in and out of this crevice, — an operation which she informed me was called 'frigging,' — keeping time to the quick prods of Father Angelo's prick in my own cunt, while she kept pushing her bottom backwards and forwards.

" 'That's a darling!' she said, with convulsive starts. 'Oh! Now its coming! — Fuck! Father! Fuck! — Push your stones hard against her arse! — Drive your fingers into my cunt, Robina, — not one but two— three—four! — All you can ! — Oh ! !'

"And she squeezed the lips of my cunt so hard that I almost screamed out, while the Father actually bellowed with delight as he poured a flood of hot sperm into my throbbing recess.

"Madame finished up by leaning over me, rubbing her bare bubbies on mine, and darting her luscious tongue into my open mouth."

"Ah! Robina!" sighed Lucia. "That was a fuck! Your charming account of it has set me wild! My cunt is just burning!" — And pulling up her skirt in front, she continued, "Look at it, darling! — Tasso is watching, too, but I don't mind. — I would give all the world for a good fuck now! — Put your hand on it and frig me, darling, and let Tasso see you."

"Lucia! Are you mad?" chided Robina. "How fortunate that the Sisters have gone in! — But we must not delay now. And see! Tasso is showing us his prick! Watch him, frigging it with his hands."

"Yes. Robina. Tasso is a dear fellow! How well he understands what to do! — Oh! How nice his prick looks! How stiffly it stands up! Wouldn't I like to have it in my cunt now ? I love to watch it while you are rubbing me there ! — Oh ! How nice ! Now faster ! — Push your fingers up ! — Oh ! ! There ! ! ! — Now let me rest, and I will go with you in a moment. "

And with a sigh she leaned her head on Robina's shoulder.

Tasso was now in great need of relief himself. He felt his balls nearly bursting with their contained charge. Satisfying himself that there was no one in the garden but themselves, he stepped nimbly up to them, his fine prick standing out before him, and boldly pushed it up close to Robina's face. She put her hand upon it, and knowing well what he wanted, drew it to her mouth. Then she placed her other hand on his balls, which were also exposed. The soft touch of her fingers on those highly sensitive organs thrilled him with delight. He thrust forward his prick, and pressed its head against her lips. They opened, and in popped the prick, and she began to suck.

He gently worked his arse backwards and forwards, and thus fucked her mouth, as if it were a cunt. She held his balls firmly, and tightened her grasp around the roots of his prick. Her pliant tongue wound around its head, while she sucked with all her force.

Then came the gushing seed, which filled her mouth even to overflowing. She held all she could until he withdrew his prick, and then ejected the slimy sperm on the grass.

Tasso smiled his thanks, and at once turned away, but they detained him long enough to make an appointment with him for the evening. With a bow he left them, after which they also speedily retired.

CHAPTER IV.

OTHER NUNS DESIRE IT

THE two young nuns succeeded in having a pleasant meeting with Tasso not only on that evening, but on some days following. And by watching their opportunity, they several times enjoyed with him their favorite sport.

As they had done their utmost to avoid attracting observation, they thought that their friendly intercourse with Tasso had escaped the notice of everyone. But as is usually the case in such matters, they were very much mistaken.

The Sisters were not permitted to form special friendships; yet when they enjoyed any freedom together, they naturally fell into pairs or sets.

There were two other nuns, named Aminda and Pampinea, who had similar tastes and usually walked together.

They observed the intimacy which had sprung up between the Sisters Lucia and Robina, and the gardener; and feeling certain that there was something in the wind, they watched him closely.

So it was arranged that Pampinea was to hide among the thick bushes by the side of the summer-house one evening, to watch and report to her friend all that she could find out.

At their next meeting, Aminda at once asked:

"Well, Pampinea, dear, what news have you?"

"Most wonderful, — beyond our wildest imagination. Frightful in one sense, delightful in another. I must begin at the very beginning."

"Yes; do, dear."

"I found a capital hiding place, where I was quite concealed, and yet, by drawing aside a branch I could see right into the summer-house. Shortly afterwards, the two Sisters, looking as innocent as a pair of doves, came and sat down. And as soon as all the others had left the garden, Tasso marched in with a broad grin upon his face. They smiled on him, and let him place them as he liked. So without losing a moment, he had them both kneeling on the seat with their ends turned out. Then he whipped up their petticoats and uncovered to view their large white bottoms.

"Then, my dear, he took out his big red 'what-you-call-it.'

"I was horrified at first, and felt ready to sink into the ground with shame, but it is odd how soon one gets accustomed to these things!

"I could not keep my eyes off it. I wondered at its size, and its great red head. Well, my dear, he pushed it up against the bottom first of the one, and then of the other.

"They had no feeling of modesty, at all, for they poked themselves out, and spread their legs apart so as to let him see all they had, — their cute little bottom-holes, hairy slits, and everything.

"He smacked their bottoms with his tool, and then pushed it all into Lucia's slit. She seemed to like it well, for she laughed as she felt it going up. But she did not hold it long, for he quickly pulled it out and shoved it into Robina in the same way.

"Then when he had given her a similar prod, he went back to Lucia, and so on from one to the other.

"All the time they were thus engaged, they continued laughing and talking to one another; and, my dear, you would hardly credit the words they used. They said that Tasso had fucked them that way before, but they thought it very pleasant. They liked to feel his hairy belly rubbing against their bottoms and that his prick seemed to get even further into their cunts than ever before. — Tell me, did you ever hear such words?"

"I did. I remember hearing them when I was a girl at school. They are coarse words, and perhaps for that very reason all the more exciting. So go on, and use them as much as you please. Your description is very amusing, — and, do you know, it is causing me a peculiarly pleasant feeling in my cunt?

You see I use them, too. — Would you mind putting your hand on it, dear, while you are describing what followed ? "

"Not in the least. I shall quite enjoy it, and you can do the same for me, for my cunt too is burning with heat. And I have had to pet it. Twice I witnessed the wonderful enjoyment which both Lucia and Robina showed, when they had Tasso's prick poking their cunts."

Then the two nuns, in very un-nun like fashion, managed to get their hands on the other's cunt as Pampinea went on:

" After changing several times, I noticed that Tasso's prick looked larger and redder each time it came out. He plunged it with great force into Sister Lucia; his belly smacked against her bottom. He remained as if glued to her behind, but Robina stood up, and pushing her hands between them, began 'fiddling with his stones and Lucia's arse,' as she called it.

"After a couple of minutes or so he drew out his prick, now all soft and hanging down, and some kind of white stuff dripping from it. Lucia then turned about and sat down, and made Tasso sit on the seat beside her, while Robina knelt on the ground before them, between Tasso's legs.

"Lucia put her hand on his balls and Robina took hold of his prick. And, my dear, she put it into her mouth, wet as it was.

"Lucia laughed: 'Ah! Robina, you are like me, — I love to taste the flavor of your cunt, and now I hope you won't find that the flavor of mine is disagreeable.'

"Robina lifted her head, and said: 'Not in the least. I like the salty taste, and the smell is delicious.'

"Then she recommenced her sucking, while Lucia's fingers played about the root of the prick, and occasionally touched the chin and sucking lips of her friend.

"Tasso's prick grew stronger, until its head seemed too large for Robina's mouth to take it all in. Lucia remarked its size and said: 'I think, Robina, that you have sucked Tasso's prick into working order again. What would you think of getting him to lie down there on his back, and then for you to straddle over him, place his prick in your cunt with your own hand? — And I will help you if you like?

Then go through the motions yourself and make him suck you at your leisure.'

" 'Capital notion! Let us at once put it into execution, for our time is nearly up.'

" They both stood up and soon had Tasso on his back on the ground. Then Robina, tucking up her skirts all around, straddled over him and made her cunt descend upon his standing prick.

"Lucia fixed it aright, and kept it steady as a candlestick with her hand, while Robina, with a downward push caused it to rush up into her to the very hilt.

"Lucia then laid herself down by Tasso's side and rested her cheek on his belly, so close to his prick that she was able to touch with her tongue at the same time both the little fleshy knot of Robina's cunt, and the prick as often as it was pressed down, while she allayed her own excitement by working a finger between the hairy lips of her own affair.

"Altogether it was a most voluptuous scene. What, between their lustful motions, their wanton cries, and the sweet visible union of prick and cunt, nothing could be more exciting. I envied them with all my heart, and I am sure, Aminda, you would have done so too. "

"I am quite certain I should, — and more. I know of no reason why we may not share in their sports — do you?   But we must go, now.   We will talk the matter over on the next opportunity. "

CHAPTER V.

LUCIA GETS MORE OF IT

E MUST now return to the two young nuns first mentioned in this narrative.

The day had come for Lucia to complete her confession to Father Joachim in the private room of the Mother Abbess. She and Robina had pledged one another, as you will doubtless remember, not to refer in any way during confession to their intercourse with Tasso, — but they agreed later that they might safely tell the priest how Lucia had seen his prick, and how they had talked together and petted each other's cunts.

Let us pass on then to the scene.

Lucia is kneeling beside the priest, who is

seated on a comfortable arm-chair in Madame's private apartments. This little room is elegantly fitted up as a lady's boudoir. It had two doors, one opening into her reception room, — the other partially concealed, led by a secret passage to the Sacristy of the Convent Chapel. And by this way, the priests who officiated there could always visit the Mother Abbess without being noticed.

What a handsome man is Father Joachim! The bloom of youth is still upon his cheek. His white untarnished skin and full red lips had made many a voluptuously-inclined maid sigh with unrequited desire. Though somewhat of a tendency to embonpoint, yet his body might be termed a veritable cushion, in which a thousand dimples hid themselves until at the proper moment they were called into action. The fame of this handsome priest had travelled before him. For his celebrated amour with an angel* was a stock story in monasteries and convents. Robina and Lucia were not unacquainted with it, the Mother Abbess having retailed the gossip previous to Father Joachim's coming.

*Lascivious Scenes in the Cloister, pages 51 — 72.

Lucia has just reached that part of her confession where she tells the priest how, having occasion to go to the Little-house, she saw through the perforated door, the gardener Tasso, coming up, unbuttoning his trousers, and taking out his tool and making water.

"Do you remember my daughter, the name you mentioned in your last confession for a man's tool ? I wish you to use it now."·

"Well, Father, if you will have me use these naughty words, it was his prick that I saw."

The priest's eyes now began to glisten, and there was a slight tremor in his hand as he said:

"Yes; it makes your confession more real and exact. Now tell me precisely all he did."

Lucia could hardly repress a smile, for she felt that she now had the priest in leading strings, and she was determined to draw him on. So she spoke out more boldly as she continued:

"When he took out his prick, he held it in his hand and shot forth his water straight before him, and he looked down on his prick while he piddled. When he finished, he shook it two or three times. Then he drew the skin back from its red head, which made it grow larger and stick out more stiffly before him."

"Now tell me, my daughter, exactly and fully what effect the view of Tasso's prick had upon yourself, and use the terms you have already uttered in confession."

"Oh! Father! How can I tell you such things?" And she leaned her elbow on his knee.

"It is quite necessary, my child, and the more particular you are in every word and in every detail the better your confession will be."

"Well, Father, I suppose I must tell you everything. — As I kept looking at the prick, I felt a warm glow all between my legs, and my cunt began to itch so terribly that I pulled up my petticoats and squeezed it with my hand. Then I pushed my finger in and rubbed the inside as hard as I could."

"Were you standing up at the time?"

"I was, Father."

"Were your legs separated?"

"They were, Father."

"Now get up, separate your legs, and stand just as you did at the time."

Lucia stood up and straddled her legs.

"I am glad to find you so true a daughter of our Holy Mother Church. — for obedience to your spiritual guides is the very essence of her teaching.

"Now put your hand on your cunt just as you did when you were looking at the gardener's prick."

Lucia lifted her clothes at one side and put her hand on her cunt. The priest looked greatly excited, and said:

" But, my daughter, I want to see it."

"Well, Father you must raise my clothes yourself."

The priest's cheeks flamed with amorous desire; and the fire of lust flamed in his eyes as he lifted her petticoats in front, and stooping forward, he was enabled to gaze upon the revealed beauties of her charming cunt. Then with a quick motion of his other hand, he rapidly unbuttoned his breeches as he said:

"Now, my daughter, that the scene may be complete, I want you to look at my prick while you are rubbing your cunt. You know these things are no sin with a holy man like me. See! Here is my prick! Look at it!"

And placing his hand behind on her naked bottom, he drew her in towards him.

The priest's burly prick, still larger and stronger than Tasso's, stood up boldly before her.

"Does the sight of this prick excite you in the same way that the gardener's did?"

"Oh! It does, Father. But are you sure it is not wrong to look at it?"

"Quite sure, my daughter, and you may put your hand on it too, without fear of sin. My child, your confidence is most refreshing. Yes, I would like you to feel it all over, — and the balls too, if you will, while I explore your delicious cunt."

Then he pushed his finger up and began to rub it quickly in and out.

"Good! My child, now come over and rest upon this lounge."

With his arm round her, he drew her to the end of the couch, laid her on her back, lifted her legs, and pushed her petticoats above her navel. He then stooped over her and with his hand directed his prick between the moist lips of her itching cunt.

As soon as she felt it in that sensitive recess, she panted out:

"Oh! Father! What do want to do?"

"To push my prick into your cunt and fuck you. Isn't that the right word to use? May I fuck you?"

"Why, Father, you told me I must obey you in everything, and if you want to fuck me, of course I must let you."

The priest smiled approval, and gave a lunge with his prick.

"Oh! It's going in! — Oh! Father! — How strong your prick is! I feel it up to the very centre of my belly! — Oh! — Do you like fucking me?"

"Yes, my daughter. Your cunt holds my prick deliciously. I have fucked many of the Sisters, but I like your cunt best of all. And especially because you talk so freely. — Now, heave your arse! — That's the way! — Now! — Oh! — It's just coming! — Put your arms around me! — Hug me! Tighter yet! Now tell me how you feel."

"Dear Father, your prick in my cunt feels lovely — I would like to keep it there forever! Fuck! Fuck! Fuck!"

The priest drove his prick up with his full force. His brawny loins smacked against the soft cheeks of her arse, and his hard balls pressed against the sensitive edges of her bottom-hole, while the flood of his fierce passion filled the recesses of her well satisfied and delighted cunt.

"Dear, dear Father!" she cries in her ecstacy. " Give me your lips to lick ! — Oh ! Blessed Virgin ! I feel your lovely prick emptying itself inside of me ! — Now I come ! I come — There ! There ! — Oh ! God ! What pleasure !"

"Yes ! Darling daughter ! Suck my mouth !" shouts the delighted priest.

Then no sound is heard except the sucking of lips and the pleasing noise made by the priest's prick as it gurgles in and out of Lucia's cunt. His prick still remained stiff, though he had spent freely. This was too much for the partly distracted Lucia. She lost control of her senses, in fact, fairly swooned away.

CHAPTER VI.

THE MOTHER ABBESS DELIGHTS IN IT

HEN she regained her senses, she looked about. The priest was gone. There was a feeling as if something were rubbing and titillating her grotto of love, and she opened her eyes wide. To her intense surprise she saw that the Mother Abbess was bending over her and she felt her fingers were playing with her dripping cunt.

"My daughter," she said, "you have behaved well. I am glad you showed such child-like obedience, and put your body to the holy service of giving relief to that worthy priest. It is no sin with him, you know, nor with me either. And I greatly commend your good sense in using all those terms which so increase and intensify these precious delights. And whenever you are with me, on similar occasions, I wish you always to use such words. I saw you fucked, my child. I was close by, when Father Joachim's prick was prodding your cunt, and I heard everything you said. Now open your legs wide. I want to kiss your cunt while it is still wet with his holy seed."

Lucia lay as if thunderstruck. She did not know what to say in reply, but she willingly spread her legs as she felt the warm breath of the Mother Abbess blowing aside the hairs of her cunt. Then she felt her soft tongue licking all round the inside of the slit, and then the whole of the clitoris drawn into her mouth. This was very enjoyable, but when she felt her tongue actually penetrating the passage, she could not resist putting down her hand, and laying it gently on the head of the Mother Abbess as she said:

"Dear Mother, how good you are! You are making my cunt glow with as much pleasure as when the Holy Father was fucking me."

The only response of the Mother Abbess was to work her tongue more nimbly in and out, and to push a moistened finger into her bottom-hole.

This last act caused a new sensation to Lucia, and made her press up against the mouth of the Mother Abbess and cry:

"Oh! My! That's so nice! Dear Mother, I am just going to spend!— My cunt and bottom are all in a glow!—Oh! Oh!— There! It's coming!"

And the Mother Abbess skilfully frigged her arse, while she lapped up with her tongue every drop of the love juice which exuded from Lucia's hot little recess.

The Mother Abbess allowed her to rest for a while, then kissed her, and said:

"I am very glad you have had so much enjoyment. Will you not do the same for me?"

"That I will, dear Mother. I am indeed longing to see and pet your dear cunt, only I was afraid to ask you."

And Lucia stood up, as the Mother Abbess took her place.

"See then, here it is!"

And laying herself back the Mother Abbess drew up her petticoats and spread her legs wide apart.

Lucia had never before seen such a cunt as that which was now opened to her view. — So large, so hairy! Such immense lips! The thick fleshy clitoris stuck out like a boy's cock! And the red chink below it was deep and bathed in moisture.

She was of course familiar with her own little chink, which was young and fresh, and had a pert and innocent air about it. And she had often seen and closely examined Sister Robina's cunt, which was fuller and more open, and had a strong lust-provoking look about it, — but even Robina's was small and poor in comparison with the great shaggy affair of the Mother Abbess. From being long in the habit of affording relief to all these burly priests, its naturally thick lips had become enormously developed, and its capacity for taking in pricks of any dimensions was unlimited. Evidently nothing could startle this woman. In fact, she never saw a jackass with his tool extended, or viewed a stallion's telescopic tickler without wishing that she had it packed in her capacious hot-box.

Such was the cunt which Lucia now stooped over. She drew open the great fat lips, and as she looked into the deep rosy chink, she thought:

"Oh! That I had a man's prick, that I might plunge into these soft folds!"

But not having the prick, she could only do what little a woman could. So she placed her mouth in the open chink, sucked the clitoris with a will, and when she had forced an emission, she began to lick up the flowing juice.

She was however, suddenly interrupted. A man's hand pushed under her chin, and gently raised her head. Looking up with surprise, she saw another of the holy Fathers, named Ambrose, standing by her side, and his prick, still larger than Father Joachim's poking against her face.

In reply to her astonished look, he said:

"Let me, my child. This is what she wants. Pleasant as no doubt your mouth and tongue are, there is nothing like the real man's prick itself. Good Mother, may I take this sweet daughter's place? If you will permit, I am ready to serve you, and she can play with my prick and balls whilst I give full satisfaction to your heated and longing cunt."

"You are very welcome, Father Ambrose. I did not expect you for another full hour yet. Give me a satisfactory poke first, and by the time you are ready again, Sister Lucia will, I am sure, gladly avail herself of the services of your noble tool."

Without delay, Father Ambrose knelt close up to her great fat rump, now flattened out on the edge of the couch.

With one fierce, rapid thrust, he buried his enormous tool in her open cunt, while she, giving the fullest swing to her randy amorous inclinations, called out,

"Now Lucia, hold his prick by the roots. Keep a firm grip on his bollocks, — his balls, you know, — and pinch his arse well. That's the way to make him fuck with life and spirit."

At each of these smutty words, the priest made a fresh plunge, and she as eagerly bounded to meet him.

Lucia gladly obeyed her Superior, and with a merry laugh pushed one hand between the Mother Abbess and the priest's hairy belly, and compressed her fingers as tightly as she could round the root of his prick. The other hand she put behind and took hold of the priest's cods, — first one and then the other, for they were too big for her hand to contain them both at once.

The holy Father now checked his speed, and, wishing to prolong the sweet joy, worked deliberately with a long steady stroke, pulling out the whole of his prick except the tip each time he drew back; while the Mother Abbess, more eager in her lust, crossed her feet over his back, and clung to him with arms and legs. But Lucia got so excited from watching his prick as it rushed in and out between the large clinging lips of Madame's voluptuous cunt, that she threw off all reserve, and pulled up her clothes and rubbed her naked cunt and belly against the firm cheeks of the priest's muscular backside. Then embacing him tightly round the loins with her arms, she joined in every push, tickling his arse most delightfully with the hair of her cunt.

This quickly brought on the climax, and the priest, with a loud exclamation of delight deluged the cunt of the Mother Abbess with his flowing sperm.

They rested a little, but with the secret parts of their bodies fully exposed, ready for either viewing or petting as might be desired.

Then the Mother Abbess produced some choice wine and spiced cakes. Each glass of wine which the good priest drank, he first seasoned by rubbing it on the cunt of one or the other, while they in like manner rubbed their glasses on his prick.

The Mother Abbess wanted them to hurry, and told Lucia to suck his prick, or do something to get him into fucking order.

He declared that if they would favor him piddling before them, it would excite him more than anything else they could do.

She laughed and said:

"Oh! I know your taste that way, and have a utensil here at hand. Come, Lucia, you must perform first, and if you piddle over his face and spurt a little into his mouth, he will be all the better pleased."

She then laid two or three folds of a large towel on the floor and said:

"Lay your head down on this, reverend Father, and Sister Lucia will place her cunt over your face and wash it with her warm piss; and if you like to open your mouth, I dare say she will please you by pissing right into it."

Lucia readily entered into the sport, and

tucking up her skirts all round, so that the whole of her belly, thighs and bottom were exposed to view, she squatted down on his face.

Then looking down between her legs, she said:

"Now Father, I am going to piss. — Are you ready?"

"Yes, daughter. Piss away, and give me a mouthful first."

Lucia, who happened to have her vessel full, spurted out its amber contents with a hissing sound and much steam right into his open mouth. Then with a slight inclination of her body, she pissed over his eyes and face, and finished in the pot which the lascivious Mother Abbess held for her convenience.

Then the Father sat up, spat out what he had taken, and rinsed out his mouth. Then wiping his face, he pointed to his prick and said:

"See how the fellow stands now!"

Then he cried:

"Don't think of drying your cunt, Lucia! I want to fuck it, while the drops of your warm piss are still hanging about it. Let me see it! — It is just right! — Now kneel here on the edge of this lounge. Lift up your arse as high as you can. And will you, good Mother, put it in for me, and while I am fucking, play with us any way you like?"

The Mother Abbess knew what was implied in that permission, and at once began to finger both their bottoms.

The priest, however, did not get in as speedily as he expected. Lucia had not as yet taken in a prick of such abnormal proportions as that of Father Ambrose, and it stuck fast in the entrance of her cunt.

"Oh!" he cried. This is grand! Her cunt is so tight that it won't let my prick in! But I like it all the more! — Does my prick hurt you, my daughter?"

"It does a little, Father. But I can bear it. — Ha! Oh! — Go softly! — Now push again! — I am trying to open my cunt for you. — There! It's getting in! Oh! Now I feel it going up! — up! — Oh! How immense it seems! I can feel it up to my very heart! My cunt is quite filled with it! Ah! Now it goes in easily enough! — Oh! Oh! That's delicious! Fuck me, Father! Fuck me! — More! More!"

She dwelt upon the word with such a libidinous accent as nearly set the priest wild, and caused him to drive his prick so forcibly in and out of her thrilling cunt as made the couch and everything movable near them vibrate with the violence of his powerful strokes.

In the meantime the Mother Abbess had worked her passions up to an almost ungovernable pitch. She was visibly spending. In her frenzy of voluptuousness she almost tore their bottoms with her nails, as she urged on their mad ecstacy until Lucia's rolling eyes and heaving bottom told of the exquisite pleasure she was experiencing. Even the priest's eyes glittered and flashed, and his whole form quivered as he poured into Lucia's womb a flood of love's soothing-syrup.

"Ha! My pretty nun! What think you now?" shouts the Mother Abbess, apparently crazed with lust. "Do you know of another joy equal to this?"

With these words she secured possession of a rod and proceeded to lay it on the bounding arses of both priest and nun.

"Nice, plump arse!" she cries, lashing Lucia's posteriors severely. "Take that! And that ! — So ! — That makes you bounce, eh ? — Now, Father, it is your turn. ''

So saying she cut the priest across the big fat cheeks of his arse so severely that he bounded like a rubber ball.

Lucia madly digs her fingers into its cheeks and holds the priest in such a firm grip that he cannot move. The Mother Abbess next gives Lucia a turn with the rod. Though the blows are quick and heavy, the girl is unmindful of them. She utters a loud shriek indicative of ecstatic pleasure. The priest expresses his blissful feelings in a pleased grunt. The Mother Abbess lays aside the rod, and then they all sank down, clutched in each other's arms.

CHAPTER VII.

IT IS THE CAUSE OF A MIRACLE

EANWHILE, our friends Pampinea and Aminda held a consultation as to the best means of securing a share of Tasso's much prized services. Of course they neither felt nor acted as ordinary women. From the forced constraint under which they lived, their passions when aroused were almost uncontrollable; and the fact of Tasso's being unable, as they supposed, to either hear or speak, induced them to regard him as more of a machine than a man, and treat him so.

It was therefore agreed that Pampinea, the bolder of the two, was to write on his slate that she had seen all that he had done to the two Sisters in the Summer-house, and to invite him to go with them and do the same.

So waiting their opportunity, Pampinea went up and held out her hand for the slate. He gave it readily.

But what was she to write? After several abortive attempts she produced the following:

"I saw you in the Summer-house with the Sisters Lucia and Robina. I saw what you were doing. It seemed to please them so much that Sister Aminda and I would like you to teach us the same delightful game. — You may trust us, we will not tell any one, — no, not even confess it to the priest."

When he read it, he looked up with an amused but very pleased expression. Pampinea smiled in return, and pointed to the Summer-house. He nodded, and motioned to her to enter it.

The two Sisters looked carefully around; and, seeing no one about, sauntered up to the place, entered, and sat down.

Tasso quickly followed them. He assumed a half-witted expression as he stood before Pampinea, scratching his head, and at the same time making the huge bulkiness of his swelling prick as prominent as he could.

With an inquiring glance, she pointed to it as if asking what it was.

Oh! How his eyes did twinkle as he took her hand and rubbed it over his tool, letting her feel how it bounded and reared in its confinement. Her fingers began to fumble with the opening of his trousers. He undid the buttons, and with a dexterous movement brought the whole length of that stately machine into view.

The Sisters started! They had never seen a man's prick displayed openly before them in that fashion. It is true that Pampinea indeed, had seen it before, but then it was in the dusk of the evening, and was always popping out of one cunt and into the other, and she remembered that when he had finally drawn it out, it had an exhausted, shrunken and crest-fallen appearance. But now it stood erect, in all the power, and all the freshness, and all the beauty of its youthful vigor.

Their eyes devour it. Their hungry little mouths of cunts began to water for it. They felt their quims throb with the first impulses of pleasure. They were quite ready even now, to fall on their backs, spread apart their legs, and allow him to fondle and view and pet their sweet treasures. They longed for that blissful moment when he should part their jutting lips, and then put in his dear prick and let it revel in the sweets within. Still, with womanly instinct they held back and let him make the first forward move, and select whichever of them he might choose to commence with.

He did not long leave them in doubt.

There was a bold dash about Pampinea which strongly attracted him. Men always admire courage in a woman, especially when it tends to confidence in themselves; and she had shown a freedom from fear, with respect to him, which was simply delightful.

Like an Eastern devotee he dropped on his knees before her, and with his hands reverently raised the coarse garment of the nun as if it were a costly veil which sheltered the object of his worship.

Having gone so far, Pampinea was not the woman to halt now. She therefore allowed him to proceed, and to act according to the instincts of his nature.

She suffered him to open her thighs, to draw her to the edge of the seat, and push her back. Then, when she felt his fingers amorously examining and probing her cunt, feeling its moist creases and soft folds, and was also conscious that his bold eyes were running over all the beauties of these secret parts, she blushed a rosy blush of pleasure from head to foot, and felt a thrill of delight pervade the regions of love, until the very lips of her cunt seemed to part in a gentle smile with the anticipation of the approaching joys.

Aminda looked on with great interest, trying to imagine how she would feel herself under similar circumstances, when she suddenly remembered that Tasso could neither speak nor hear, and so she said,

"Dear Sister, don't you feel terribly ashamed at his looking at you there?"

"Not at all, dear," replied Pampinea. "Strange to say, I don't mind it in the least. I really like it now, — it seems so natural."

"Well," said Aminda, "it may be quite natural; but at first — well, at all events — it does look very queer. Anyhow, I feel that I would love to watch what he is doing to you forever. You don't dislike it, Pampinea, do you, dear?"

"No. I like you to watch. — Oh! Now I feel him rubbing against me that part which Lucia called his prick, and I can't tell you, dear, how nice it feels! He's trying to get it in now! — Oh! It's hurting me a little. But the pleasure is just maddening. Oh! Aminda! He's just got it in! — Now the pain is over, and he has pushed it all up, it feels delightful! — I cannot tell you how delicious it is, now that he is moving it in and out! Can you see it, dear?"

"Oh! Yes! — I see it plainly enough! — How easily it slips in and out! — It must indeed feel very nice! My own cunt, — at least that's what Lucia and Robina called theirs —"

"Well! — What about your cunt, my dear?"

"Oh! My cunt is tingling all over at the sight! — I do hope Tasso will like mine as as he likes yours. Oh! How delicious it must feel to be fucked! — Is n't that the word?"

"Yes! — Oh! I can't talk now. — Fucking is delightful. — No terms — can — express — how — delicious — it feels!"

These words were uttered in successive

jerks as Tasso drove in and out his red and swollen tool, while the hungry lips of her quivering cunt sucked it in with all the eagerness of the highest and voluptuous enjoyment.

Aminda shared their transports, and putting her hand on her own itching slit, forced her finger for the first time up the thrilling passage of her cunt.

"Tell me now, Pampinea, how do you feel?" cried Aminda, vigorously working her excited cunt.

"I — I — Oh!   You heavenly man! — I must move my backside, too! — Don't ask me, Aminda! It's just too sweet to talk about! — Oh! I am all wet inside of me! — But you won't take it out, will you?" she pleadingly asks of Tasso, forgetful of his being powerless to hear.

"His prick is covered with oil," remarked Aminda. "I guess he must be nearly done. — At least I hope so," she adds, in a slightly petulant tone.

Tasso was now fucking the long-deprived maid with all his strength. His finely developed prick was as stiff as ever; and every time he thrust it in to the full, Pampinea uttered little shrieks of delight. At last he made a quick thrust, and buried his prick in the anxious and longing cunt to its fullest extent, and then ceased his motions.

"Oh! Aminda!" cried Pampinea. "He is squirting hot streams into me!—Oh! Oh! There he goes again! Oh! I can not tell you of the sweet, sweet feeling that is within me. I only wish he would not take it out! I want it right over again!"

"That is indeed unkind of you, Pampinea," said Aminda, poutingly. "You know I have been fingering my cunt until I am almost mad with desire. Come, now! Do let me have a taste of what you have just felt."

While she was speaking these words, Tasso withdrew himself from Pampinea's luscious cunt. The fact was, all this fucking was beginning to tell a little upon the gardener's vitality. Yet such was the tempting nature af the feast which was being constantly spread before him that, to save his soul, he could not resist the offerings.

Pampinea was wildly excited by the workings of Tasso's prick. She still imagined that something was working within her, for after Tasso had take his prick from her, she continued the motions just as though she were again being fucked.

The gardener now turned his attention to Aminda, who was eagerly awaiting her turn. She certainly was a very beautiful woman, and as fresh and sweet as a full blown rose. The red blood mantled her cheek; her lily white skin was without a flaw. Her eyes were aflame with passion. Her position was such as to expose her most secret charms, the sight of which instantly made Tasso's prick arise once more.

"Do you like to look at my cunt?" inquired Aminda artlessly upon the slate.

Tasso nods his head vigorously.

"I love to look at your prick," she again writes.

This breathing spell gave Tasso a splendid opportunity to raise a stiff prick. He knew that he had spent heavily in Pampinea, and the result would be that his staff when it once hardened again, would remain stiff for quite a period. As he saw his prick become as hard as a stone, he could not contain himself any longer. The sight of Aminda's pouting little love-nest added to his joy.

Then he fell upon his knees between the plump white thighs, and exclaimed:

"Oh! Mother of God! What a glorious feast!"

As he spoke each word, he greedily kissed Aminda s quivering cunt.

"He speaks! He speaks!" cries Pampinea, awakened to herself at the sound of Tasso's voice.

But the gardener paid no attention to her. He saw only Aminda and her secret beauties. He opens the lips of her anxious cunt, and pushes his big stiff prick right into her without heeding either her cries or her protestations.

The girl's cries however, were not unheard by others. The Mother Abbess and Father Joachim, who were indulging in a little stroll through the grounds, were attracted to the Summer-house by such unseemly noises.

And what a sight it was that greeted their eyes!

There was Pampinea, lying upon the ground, with disordered attire, and vigorously rubbing the clitoris and stiffened inner lips of her still slippery cunnie, while not far from her, Tasso and Aminda were battling right royally in amorous warfare.

"By the Great God above!" shouts the intoxicated Tasso. "That was a fine return! — Ha! Ha! There is another for thee! Now, Now! My beautiful angel, give it back right quickly!"

"A miracle! A miracle!" shouts the Mother Abbess. "The dumb speak, and the deaf hear! Bear witness to this wondrous thing, Father Joachim!"

"Aye! Aye!" returns Father Joachim. "This must go upon the records. It will be recorded for all time in order to confound the erring ones and doubters. By Saint Anthony!" he shouts. "But that fellow fucks like a master of the art."

" 'T is a most entrancing sight!" observes the Mother Abbess, watching the two with amorous eyes. "How fortunate I am to witness it," she continues.

Pampinea in the meantime had arisen, and after arranging her attire, stood with downcast eyes and flushed cheeks awaiting her sentence. The Mother Abbess however did not pay any attention to her, and acted as though she was unaware or Pampinea's presence.

"Ha! That was an excellent shove!" she shouts. "Now, Aminda, return it with

interest. Hold! I will stroke his arse, and
fondle his balls. Now! Now! Gardener,
show your mettle!"

Pampinea was overjoyed to witness the
Mother Abbess' actions. She now felt more
secure as she observed the conduct of her
Superior.

With his arse being slapped, his balls
fondled, and his prick tightly enfolded in an
hitherto unfucked cunt, Tasso was in the
seventh heaven of bliss. Nature could hold
back no longer.

"Come! Come!" cried Father Joachim.
"Spit the contents of thy loins into the maid.
This will but half satisfy her. By Saint
Anthony! I will take a hand in the game
myself."

The priest was right. When Tasso removed
himself Aminda endeavored to prevent it.

"What! Through already?" she cried,
regardless of the company. "Bah! I am
but half satisfied! — Oh! Holy Virgin! —
Give me a prick! I am burning up with
desire."

Aminda was in that state of feeling that few
physicians seem acquainted with. The most
modest and virtuous woman, left in an

unsatisfied state, would without reluctance yield herself to the embrace of her most hated foe. 'Tis now that Father Joachim finds the best field for the display of his unrivalled talents.

"Fuck her, Father! Fuck her!" cried the amorous Mother Abbess. "Tasso is dry."

The gardener was highly indignant at the thrust.

"Madame," he retorts, "were you in my place, and beseeched constantly by a dozen prick-hunters such as your nuns here, upon my soul you would not have another drop within you."

"Ha! Ha!—Nice carryings on in my convent," remarks the Mother Abbess in a serio-tragic tone. "You are the deaf and dumb man, eh?—The modest one who dared not raise your eyes in passing us, eh?—By the Blessed Mother, I will have you to fuck me and no one else,—dost hear?"

"Alas! Madame," returns Tasso. "I pray you have mercy! You know the old saying, that 'one cock will do for ten hens, but one prick will not do for a dozen women,' for be it known to you that ten stiff pricks cannot satisfy one woman. Know you also that a

disorder of long standing had deprived me of
hearing as well as speech. The beautiful
Aminda gave me such extreme pleasure that
my senses were for a time dissapated. When
they returned, I found myself a perfect man
again.''

"We will speak further of this in the
future," said the Mother Abbess. "Just now
we have no further time to waste on thee. —
Ha! Observe Father Joachim!—See! He
has already replaced thee. How well his
handsome prick fits into Aminda's little cunt!
— Watch them fuck!— Oh! Is it not an
entrancing sight? — Ho! Father! Work thy
loins! — Ha! I know you are shooting into
her. Halt her screams! Stifle them, or we
may have unwelcome visitors!''

Father Joachim was enjoying himself to the
fullest extent. Aminda's slit was eager for a
prick, and when the Father placed his splendid
tool into the hot and luscious cunt, it was
indeed, the extreme of happiness for both.
What a glorious sight it was! And how they
all enjoyed it!

When Father Joachim had spent copiously
into Aminda, he removed his fallen prick, and
dropping on his knees between her thighs,

pressed unnumbered kisses upon her still excited and palpitating cunt.

"The hour is late," spoke up the Mother Abbess. "Father, it is time to cry halt. You may enjoy this more in the future. — Tasso, away to your employment. — Pampinea and Aminda, go to your apartments."

"Were it not for an important engagement elsewhere," interrupted Father Joachim, "I would give you each such a rounding up as would make you utter shrieks of joy once more."

"Well," joined in the Mother Abbess. "in a few days we will hold high revelry, and participate in such a feast as you have never heretofore dreamed of."

A loud cry of approval greeted this bit of interesting information.

"I will inform you as to it at the proper time. — Oh! By the way, I might mention that letters have been sent from Madrid informing me that the famous Monk Pedro has been appointed one of our Confessors, and is now on the way here. I expect him the coming morrow. Rumor saith that he has been sent abroad as a punishment for engaging in an illicit amour with the King's

daughter. — I am anxious to test his abilities.
— Now, farewell.''

Speaking thus the Mother Abbess and
Father Joachim slowly wended their way
conventward, while Tasso departed to resume
his tasks.

Pampinea and Aminda walked towards their
respective apartments slowly and with a
somewhat halting gait, due no doubt to a little
too-much of that pleasant prick-rubbing to
which they had just been subjected.

CHAPTER VIII.

THEY ALL TAKE A HAND IN IT

ONVENT life in Italy at the period upon which our narrative touches, was anything but one made up of sacrifice, penance and devotion. The cloak of religion was but a thin disguise for the greatest immorality, and the greater the reputation for sanctity, the deeper would the inmates plunge into lecherous pleasures. The convent was the resort of the gay and dissolute youth of the sunny clime, who indulged in orgies and dissipation that would have done no discredit to their Roman ancestors, who had long been acknowledged by those competent to decide, to be veritable adepts in the arts of fucking, sucking and buggering. The ancients practically made the science of fucking a fine art, and we who follow ih their footsteps are naught but mere imitators. It therefore will not cause a shock to the intelligent reader to describe at length the riotous orgie which we are about to depict, for such sensual banquets were quite common in Italy, where the hot blood courses through the veins with lightning speed, and the passions at times become so uncontrollable as to rage with the fierceness of beasts or fabled centaurs.

The Convent in which the scenes of our story lay was an exception to the rule. It possessed an enviable reputation for sanctity and was frequently quoted as an example well worthy of imitation. The larger portion of its inmates confined themselves to sacred practices only, and the fall from grace of the Mother Abbess and the younger Sisters was totally unknown.

The Mother Abbess deferred to a week later the promised feast of love.

"It will give us time to recuperate," she said to Father Joachim, who impatiently awaited the evening of joy. "That fellow Tasso has been too devoted a follower of Venus," she added, with a suggestive smile.

"Hum! Lucky dog!" said the priest, a little enviously. "He is a fine gardener! — Ha! Ha!" he laughed. "What a nice crop of brats he will leave behind him! He has planted his seed to good advantage."

"I esteem it a misfortune that I was not acquainted with his talents before," observes the Mother Abbess. "But come! I must send you on a mission. Go and bid Robina, Lucia, Pampinea and Aminda to assemble here in this room to-morrow night. — Oh! By the way, forget not our Tasso. Ambrose is already informed, — and likewise the Spanish monk, Pedro."

"Why, he has but recently come from Madrid. What know you of him?"

"He is known as the Spanish Stallion, and I am informed that none can excel him in the gentle arts of love. By our Lady! I am anxious to test his virility. I already burn and itch with desire. Oh! I must play with your prick a moment, Father."

In compliance with this request, the priest undid his cassock; and showed to the amorous woman his ponderous engine.

She seizes it with greedily lustful hands, and works it fiercely, squeezing the heavy balls. At the same time Father Joachim buries his finger in her moist crevice, and they give each other exquisite pleasure for an extended period.

Finally the Mother Abbess recovers herself.

"We must not be backwards to-night," she says, giving his prick a last gallop.

Father Joachim then departed without any further delay.

Punctually at the appointed time they all assemble in the apartment selected for the meeting. The place chosen was a room in the most unfrequented portion of the Convent. Heavy curtains hid everything from prying eyes. A banquet table, spread with delicacies and luscious fruits first met the gaze of those who entered. The Mother Abbess was seated on a throne-like chair at the head of the table, and bade a most generous welcome to every guest.

"I introduce to you, ladies and gentlemen, (for that is what I will term you this festive night,) the Monk Pedro, also called the Spanish Stallion."

Shouts of laughter greet this sally.

"I will tell you my opinion when I taste his prick," observes the virtuous Robina.

"Yes! So will we all!" chime in the other psuedo-virgins.

Soon the wine was becoming effective, for all were presently partaking freely of the generous juice of the grape.

Modesty was quickly thrown aside with the vestments. The Mother Abbess was the first to set the example. A single motion, and she was entirely disrobed. One naked leg is placed upon the table. Then she falls back, sighing,

"Come, my Spanish Stallion! Fuck me before them all."

The handsome Pedro, a tall Hercules as it were, strips himself in a trice and displays a tool worthy of his title.

"Has he not a fine prick, Robina," says Lucia, admiringly. "I would very much like to feel it inside of me!"

"I am anxious to taste of it like yourself, Lucia," returns Robina, gazing with tender looks upon the Spaniard's prick.

Meanwhile the Mother Abbess was snatching frantically at the object before her. She would squeeze it gently, then draw her hand slowly backward in a most teasing manner.

The monk was pawing at her cunt in a most

ferocious way. His whole hand grasped the fat lips, and pressed them tightly. Then he would insert two fingers, and titillate her clitoris until her arse jumped convulsively.

"They are getting in fine shape for a good fuck," says Father Ambrose, taking Lucia up on his lap and inserting his stiff prick between her naked thighs. Then with his other hand, he played with Robina's cunt.

Father Joachim had placed himself in front of Pampinea's lovely font, and rapturously kissed the ruby lips.

Tasso, whose stomach was filled with good wine, seemed to be in fine fettle. His hand strayed to that delightful slit belonging to Aminda.

"That's right! Play with my cunt, dear Tasso, while I look at Father Pedro. See!" she cries. "He is about to fuck her now. Will it not be delightful for you to play with my cunt while they are fucking?"

The Mother Abbess now lost all sense of womanly modesty, for she caught hold of the Spanish Stallion's prick and pulled him by it to a couch conveniently placed, he playing with her cunt all the while. Look! She wrestles with him, twines her limbs about him

like a vine, then she falls upon the couch and
raises her limbs in the air. His mighty prick
enters her veteran cunt without a halt. With
a fierce wrench she throws him off, pounces
upon his prick with her mouth, and mumbles
her prayers over it as though Priapus were
her God.

"Have at her, Monk!" gleefully shouts
Father Ambrose.

"Hey! Stallion, your mighty prick will be
conquered this time!" cries Father Joachim.

"Yea! Yea!" chimes in Tasso. "If she
does not fuck you dry, she will suck you
dry!"

Monk Pedro was oblivious to such jesting.
He is wild with lust. He plays with his
companion's splendid arse. He pushes up her
ponderous titties, — squeezes, bites and sucks
them.

The entranced Abbess is not a whit behind.
Her tongue licks everything with which it
comes in contact.

Again his prick enters her cunt. This time
he will not be thrown off. He joins his
stomach to hers. His big balls are close to her
arse-hole. He keeps his prick in place, and
moves his muscular arse from side to side.

The Mother Abbess gasps with pleasure. She cannot speak, but utters little shrieks expressive of the exquisite pleasure she is experiencing.

"See! See! He will not be halted," says Pampinea, whose arse is already quivering with delight from Father Joachim's ravishing fingering.

In vain the partly distracted Mother Abbess motions to her partner to move in and out.

"Beloved friend," observes Father Pedro, "I have her impaled, and as I am not yet ready to spend, I will stay as I am."

"By all the Saints!" shouts Ambrose. "If you will not oblige her, I will take a turn myself."

"An excellent suggestion," rejoins the Stallion.

Then he works his arse swiftly until his prick is steaming with the juices of his partner. He then withdraws his instrument, as stiff as ever.

Father Ambrose takes his place, and the Mother Abbess engulphs his prick at a single push. He rages like a bull; their bellies meet with a loud slap. Her tongue wags at him as an invitation to his own. Now they fuck with their mouths as well. His lunges are fiercely lustful, but he is not so well primed as Father Pedro. Off comes Father Ambrose with a mighty shout of unrestrained excessive bliss.

He withdraws his flabby prick and is pushed aside by the Spaniard, who again inserts his fine mettlesome steed into the willing cunt before him. He places a finger in her arse-hole and now works his backside with wonderful speed. Again she wags her tongue. He obeys the signal.

"His time is not far off!" cries Tasso.

"Nor is mine!" cries Aminda, whose clitoris is now in fine shape to be rubbed by a stiff prick.

Robina, Lucia and Pampinea are in like condition. They were all in such a state of sexual excitement that at the slightest motion, they all would have sucked their partners' pricks without a single note of protest.

"Fuck me harder!" shrieks the Mother Abbess. "Run your finger further up my arse, and work it up and down in time with your prick. Oh! Do you never mean to spend?—Hurry! I am dying to suck your cock! Now work your finger in my arse

faster! That's it! That's something like it!
— Ha! You spend at last! — Jesu! What a
stream comes from you!"

"Ah! By Saint Iago!" shouts the now
enraptured Monk. "I am spending! I will
not lose a single drop to save your soul from
perdition!"

Saying this he gave his body a violent
wrench, followed by another and still more
violent one.

"Once more!" he shouts, shooting his
manly offerings into the innermost recesses of
her palpitating womb.

Then he glued himself to his partner, and
remained motionless for quite a period.

While the two were thus engaged, the
others were by no means idle. Father Joachim
had slipped his prick into Pampinea's tight
little cunnie, and was pushing forward and
backward in the pleasantest style imaginable.

"Your prick feels heavenly!" sighs his
partner, embracing him in the most fervid
manner.

"Yes, my daughter," he rejoins. "And
your cunt is so tight and warm that I wish I
could fuck it a whole day. Is it not delicious?
— Now suck my lips and I will suck yours! —

That is the way!—Now gurgle your tongue
in my mouth!—I feel you spending, but that
will only make you anxious to be fucked
harder."

"Oh! Father! Just look at my cunt," says
Pampinea. "See! Its lips are right against
your hair. If your prick was larger I could
take it all in with ease."

"Yes, my daughter. It is indeed a pretty
sight. Now I will not move my prick, but just
put my hands across your arse and press you
tightly to me. Ah! God!—But this is
heavenly! I will lay you down on the couch
in a few moments, and fuck you hard,—very
hard. I can now feel my prick moving gently
away up!"

"Oh! Father! I want a good hard fucking!
But before you commence, thrust your tongue
way into my mouth. There! Yes! That is
the way!—Yum! Yum! Yum!—Now fuck
me as hard as you are able!"

Father Joachim at once obeyed the anxious
girl's request. He laid her on the couch, and
gave it to her in heroic style. His fine prick
would come out only to be eagerly sucked
back by Pampinea's greedy cunt.

While thus engaged, the Mother Abbess had

placed Pedro's fallen prick in her lecherous mouth, and was sucking it with the appetite of a hungry beast.

"A prick! A prick!" she mumbles. "A prick to fuck me!"

Gentle remonstrances come from the rest of the fair ones. For as the reader knows, there were not quite enough pricks to go round, and each one was in great demand.

Father Ambrose appeared to have his nose in Robina's cunt, while his two hands were playing with Lucia's arse and crotch as well.

"I am suffering!" shrieks the Mother Abbess. "Hasten! Oh! Hasten! I am burning up!"

Father Ambrose could not resist the appeal. He now left Robina and Lucia, and placed himself between the thighs of the Mother Abbess. Her cunt was all wet with sexual dew, but this only excited the priest onward. A lecherous cry came from him. His large and thick tool was as stiff as a rod of ivory, and in fine shape to satisfy a wanton woman. With a vigorous shove, he placed his prick home and then started to fuck with all his power.

"Ah!" cries Aminda to Tasso. "The

Mother Abbess is in heaven. Look at her eyes! She appears to be enjoying herself beyond expression. She has one prick in her mouth, and another in her cunt."

"Yes!" returns Tasso, who was fucking Aminda vigorously all the while. "She ought to have something in her arse-hole, too."

"Oh! Tasso!" cries Aminda. "Turn me on my side, and then I can see the Mother Abbess being fucked whilst you fuck me."

Tasso at once complied with the request. He proceeded to give her a good prick-drubbing as she watched the others. He gave it to her so finely that Aminda's arse trembled like a leaf in the storm.

"When you get through, I must suck your prick, too," says the sobbing girl.

Tasso was also greatly excited, for as he looked about him, he saw the handsome Joachim withdraw himself from Pampinea's slit and place his prick, after bathing it in cold water, in Pampinea's mouth. She sucked it with the gusto of a child eating sweets. Robina and Lucia, left to themselves, were tickling each other's clitoris.

Tasso, with his prick in Aminda's cunt, lifted her up, and carried her to where the

Mother Abbess was engaged in amorous warfare. Placing the palpitating form of his partner in close proximity to the double fucked Abbess, he ran his finger up her arse and moving it in and out of the darker fringed hole, violently fucked Aminda at the same time.

Meanwhile Pedro's prick, under the tender manipulation of the Mother Abbess' mouth, had assumed its most formidable appearance. When he withdrew his staff, it was red and swollen.

"Put it in my arse-hole," pleads the Mother Abbess, sick with lust. "Fuck my arse-hole! — Oh! For Christ's sake, fuck it!"

As she spoke, Father Ambrose uttered a hoarse shout, and emptied into her a copious supply of rich semen. He then proceeded to suck her mouth, whilst she ran her tongue down his throat.

Aminda now commenced to move her arse with quickened motions, expressive of unalloyed pleasure; for Tasso's fine prick was touching her to the very quick.

"Hurry, Tasso!" she whispered in his mouth. "I am crazy to suck your dear prick."

While she was thus speaking, Father Pedro

flatly refused to obey the Mother Abbess' request.

"Two fine cunts are awaiting a prick!" he exclaimed. "I prefer cunt to arse-hole. Therefore, let Tasso's finger answer."

He spoke truly.

Robina and Lucia were reposing naked in each other's arms.

"Oh! I would give the world for a good prick," sighed Robina.

"So would I!" echoed Lucia.

The Spaniard at once went to them. Then placing their cunts on a level with his mouth, he cried,

"By Saint Peter! What glorious cunts! See this one with its jutting lips and scarlet mouth!—Ah! God! What a feast!"

He places his finger in Robina's wet cunt, and epicurean-like he rubbed and felt its satiny softness.

"Oh! What pleasure will I enjoy as I fuck this creamy thing! Sister Lucia, sit up on the couch! Open your thighs wider, and I will suck your cunt as I fuck Robina."

Placing a pillow under Robina's arse, he inserted his prick between the lips of her cunt, at the same time sucking Lucia's slit.

"Dear! Dear! Father!" cried Robina. "Your prick is thick and big!—But it feels perfectly heavenly!—See! You are nearly half-way in!—Oh! Merciful Saviour! It is all the way in! Now your big balls are against my arse!"

"You are indeed enjoying it, Robina, for you show by your countenance that your pleasure is very great.—Oh! Robina! He is sucking my cunt deliciously. Oh! Oh!—I will spend right in his mouth soon."

But Robina was speechless with the pent up bliss. The splendid prick of the Spanish Stallion was giving her the most exquisite joys on this earth. Her vagina sucked it so hard that Pedro could not stroke her quickly:—for when he drew his prick outward, the folds of her lovely cunt came with it, thus giving him indescribable pleasure. As he gazed about he also saw scenes that goaded him to the extremest point of human endurance.

Pampinea and Father Joachim had their hands between each other's thighs and a finger in their respective arse-holes. The Mother Abbess was busily engaged in sucking Father Ambrose's prick, whilst he, in turn, sucked wildly away at Aminda's hot and quivering cunt. On her part, she had Tasso's prick in her mouth, and was moulding it in the most lecherous manner. Tasso had his three fingers in the Mother Abbess' slit, and another finger in her arse-hole. Thus the entire company were now engaged in bestowing upon one another the most libidinous touches.

Lechery was rampant. Prick was king and Cunt was his consort. Here were men of great talents, and celebrated as teachers of the people. Their preachings electrified their hearers. They were looked upon as the servants of God deputed to do His will on this earth. No thoughts of an evil character were ever supposed to have strength enough to wean them for a moment from their priestly ways.

Yet look upon them! — Yea, behold them! — Where is now their boasted strength to resist temptation? Bah! Cunt conquers all men. And the saintly women, to whom a few months since the very thought of contact with man was contamination! — Now they are sucking pricks with the greatest gusto.

Lo! The pride of woman falleth before Prick. When priest and nun throw off the mask of sanctity, they display passion raging beneath with volcanic force. Fucking is but the half way post; sucking is another quarter, and buggering marks the finish.

When the Spanish Stallion had finished Robina, the nun was but partly satisfied. She commenced rolling forward and backward along the floor, gesticulating violently with both legs and arms.

Lucia was spending, and at the same time uttering deep sighs indicative of extreme desire. Her cunt had been well sucked but not yet fucked. A good stiff prick was now an absolute necessity to ease her sufferings.

Pedro saw her anxiously eyeing his prick. He understood her mute appeal. Then, after bathing his tool with fresh cool water, he placed it in her mouth. As he did so, she uttered little shrieks of delight. Finally, her suckings gave him the desired hard-on, and when he removed it from between her lips, it appeared bigger and thicker than ever.

She eyed it with the look of a famished hound, and threw her legs upward, thus exposing the blonde-haired cunnie, plump arse, and broad white thighs.

With a beastly cry the Spanish Stallion falls upon her, and plunges his prick straight into the close-mouthed red-limned mount of Venus, and works his arse without mercy. The greedy cunt takes it all in, and Lucia moves her arse from side to side, and meanwhile utters deep sighs of satisfaction.

"Spare me not, Father!" she cries. "Now fuck all you can! I feel your prick way up in me!"

"Sweet angel!" replies Pedro. "Was ever a man so blessed? Your cunt is so tight and warm that the head of my prick feels as if it were afire. Ah! Christ! Christ! — How I would like to put my balls into you! — Come here, Robina! Let me suck your cunt while I fuck Lucia."

Robina places herself in a position to gratify the lecherous priest, and soon he is sucking away for dear life. His big prick at the same time, is rushing in and out of Lucia's greedy cunt, with speedy thrusts.

The whole apartment now resounded with shouts of vulgar language.

"A prick for my arse-hole!" still pleads the Mother Abbess.

Alas for her! No sodomite is there to

gratify her.   There are too many enticing cunts in opposition.

Such scenes as we now depict may seem as unreal as they are unnatural; but the keen student of human nature knows well that the most modest of women, when over-excited by a good fucking, will halt at nothing.   In their cooler moments, they would be horrified at the very thought, rather than act in the manner in which the present pages now suggest.

CHAPTER IX.

A PRINCESS HAD TO HAVE IT

FOR A short period the company halted. Over-excited nature now demanded a brief respite. Through the forethought of the Mother Abbess, utensils for ablution were plentiful. Priests and nuns could be seen gently bathing pricks and cunts in order to strengthen them for renewed orgies. Wines and light refreshments abounded. Naked forms sat around the banquet board. Shafts of wit with pointed allusions brought forth paroxysms of laughter.

"The arse-hole is still waiting!" shouts Ambrose. "Who will be the first to storm the breach?"

"Yes! Yes!" returns the Mother Abbess.

(The wine-glass had been raised perhaps too often to her lips.) "I will take a prick in my mouth, another in my cunt, and still another in my arse-hole!"

"Be not so greedy!" cry the others, indignantly. "Would you deprive us all to gratify yourself?"

"Have no fear, fair Sisters," interjects Joachim. "It would take a regiment to gratify our Mistress. She is a veritable succubus. 'More! More!' is her ever constant cry."

A shout of laughter greets this sally.

"Cunts were formed for fucking, and pricks were made to fuck them!" chimes in Father Pedro. "If it were not so, God would have given us little holes to piss out of. But arse-holes were made for still another purpose, and I for one, have no desire to put my tool in such a dirty place!"

"Bravo! Bravo!" shout the anti-sodomites approvingly.

The Mother Abbess laughed loud and mockingly, in a perfect fit of mirth.

Father Joachim endeavored to restrain the outburst.

"Madame, I beseech you not to give away

to your feelings in such loud tones. We may awake the aged Sisters."

"Quiet your fear," returned the Mother Abbess, restraining her mirth somewhat. "Think you that I have not prepared against such an event? We are now in the unused portion of the Convent. The other Sisters are locked securely in their cells."

[Fathers Joachim, Pedro and Ambrose, be it known to you, were not residents of the Convent. They were supposed to dwell in a monastery some distance removed from their present location. Their vocation as Confessors however, gave them special privileges, and as the reader will observe, they were by no means backward in taking advantage of the opportunities offered them.]

The entire company now became lost to all sense of shame. Once more modesty was thrown to the winds. For wine and full stomachs have a tendency to influence the passions; and the present instance was no exception to the rule.

Would that a painter's skilled hand could depict in glowing colors what the pen is now incapable of fully describing. The beautiful maidens are now mere animals. Plump white thighs were partly lolling on the table and chairs, the atmosphere being so balmy that nakedness was pleasant. Pouting cunts were displaying themselves in such a manner as would have influenced even a hermit, or corrupted a saint, — and the Fathers present were neither. Their hands were playing with the tempting lips and clitoris of each. Deep sighs indicative of exquisite pleasure came from all. Pricks and balls were being handled in the most lascivious manner. Lily-white arses were gently rising up and down in the anticipation of the joys that were to come.

"Ah!" said Father Pedro, whose sturdy tool and large rounded appendages were worked at once by Robina and Lucia. "This is almost as fine as my palace experiences."

This remark attracted the attention of all.

"You excite our curiosity," chimes in the Mother Abbess. "Come, tell us the story. From whence comes your title of Stallion?"

"Yes! Yes!" cry the rest in unison. "Tell us the story."

Father Pedro smiled.

"I will relate to you the cause of the title," he replied. "But soft! Before I commence, sweet Sisters," he added, turning to Lucia

and Robina, "restrain your eagerness. Handle
me gently, and I will entertain each of your
cunts in return. This pleasant dalliance must
last until I finish my tale."

Then the entire company, whilst dallying
with one another, listened to the following
narrative:

"I scarcely need remind you," commenced
the narrator, "that for ages the Spaniards
have been renowned as adepts in the arts of
love as well as of war. Hot blooded and
impulsive, addicted to strong jealousies, it is
said of us that we are more prone to punish
than to reward. A Spaniard will imperil his
life and honor for a woman's embrace, yet he
will pursue with implacable vengeance the
outrager of his domestic hearth. He receives
but will make no return. Secrecy is safety—
discovery is ruin."

"Bah!" interrupted Father Ambrose.
"Have done with such dry details. Come to
the point without so much wandering."

Pedro flushed deeply at the reproof, if such
it might be termed. But an extra jerk of his
prick by Robina restrained his temper.

"Know then, that in Madrid I was in the employ of his Eminence the Cardinal, as Secretary. My employment brought me frequently to the Palace, and it was not long before I was on excellent terms with the King and the entire royal family.

"My conduct was of the most exemplary character; and I was looked upon as a model of propriety. Such was the confidence displayed in me that I became a depository for all the secrets of the Palace. I acted the part of Confessor to the best of my ability, and reproved and rewarded in turn.

"One afternoon I was summoned to the Cardinal's private apartments, and to my great astonishment, was addressed as follows:

" 'Father Pedro, you know that we who serve the Holy Father obey him in all things, halting not to inquire the why and wherefore. Therefore, my son, be not amazed at what I now speak of to you. Learn that the Princess Dolores, the fairest maid in all Spain, is in a delicate situation. Her physician informs me that she must perforce have sexual connection without delay, or her life may pay the forfeit. —Do you follow me?'

" 'Perfectly, your Eminence,' I replied.

" 'Well,' continued the Cardinal, 'a month hence she will be married to the Prince of Parma. But pending that period, her condition is so serious that nothing but a man can alleviate it. Now the marriage of the Prince and the Princess is of absolute importance, for the reason that the Church will vastly benefit by it. Should the death of the Princess prevent such a consummation, the Holy Father will be overwhelmed with grief. He has set his heart upon this union, as vast interests can thus be maintained. — But, enough of explanations. I now order you to go to the Princess this very evening, and give her that relief which nature so strenuously demands. We know we are safe when we confide in thee. We dare not seek another. What sayest thou, my son?'

" 'To hear is to obey,' I responded humbly, with head bowed and raised hands clasped in prayer.

"With a gesture, the Cardinal dismissed me.

"Now laugh as you will, Brothers and Sisters. Nevertheless, I speak truth when I state that heretofore I had never enjoyed a woman, save in imagination. You well know," he added, with a suggestive smile, "that our text-books which we striplings studied before our entrance into the priesthood, are crowded with descriptive and alluring suggestions. A hundred or more volumes are devoted solely to subjects of a sexual nature, and I can assure you that they can with truth be termed 'An Exposition of the Art of Fucking' in every shape, manner, and form known to civilized and uncivilized nations.

"The maiden I was about to satisfy was the most beautiful woman in Spain. The young gallants of Madrid would have periled their lives and fortunes to obtain her. Yet here was I offered this luscious fruit without an effort."

"Lucky dog!" quoth Ambrose, between his set teeth. "How I envy you!"

A murmur of disapproval quieted the interloper. It was evident that the company were becoming greatly interested.

"I prepared myself fittingly for the coming event," resumed Father Pedro. "The perfumed bath of the King was at my disposal that evening; for upon my arrival at the

Palace, a lovely maid of honor met me and conducted me to that apartment.

"'I have been commanded by high authority,' quoth she, with a smile upon her lovely face, ' not to lose sight of thee until the destination is reached.'

"And you may be assured she obeyed her commands faithfully. She saw me disport naked in the bath. With gloating looks did she observe my manly beauties, and it was only with great difficulty that she could restain herself from fondling me.

"When I entered the private chamber of the Princess, I saw the beautiful being reposing on a couch of great magnificence. Two maids of honor were in attendance upon her.

" Previous to my entrance I had not allowed my thoughts to dwell on the subject. I saw only the path of duty. Passion had not yet commenced to play its part.

" The Princess was attired in a silken robe; but when I fell upon my knees I saw that it covered nakedness only. For when she gave me her hand to kiss, the robe revealed the superb bosom entire to my gaze. By all the saints!" cried the enraptured Pedro. "Never did I see such a beautiful being! Her white skin would have matched the purest alabaster. Her long black hair fell to her feet. Her coal black eyes pierced me like an arrow's dart. Her cheeks were suffused with the deepest crimson, and her reddened lips were a Cupid's bow, wet with dew.

"I fell upon those lips like a famished dog. I sucked and sucked the velvet mouth, and was sucked in return, for the Princess was overflowing with desire.

" 'Pardon my sin, Father,' she whispered softly.

" 'The Virgin herself would atone for thee! —Oh! Lovely Princess,' I returned.

"Regardless of the arch-looks of the maids of honor present, I threw off my single garment. The Princess in turn imitates me, and there, naked and palpitating, does she lie before me. With eager hands I seize upon the hemispheres before me, and mumbling cries of excited lust as I press and fondle them, and suck their virgin rubies, and press unnumbered kisses alternately on lips and bosom; while she, with both hands upon my gloriously stiffened prick, is uttering cries indicative of unbridled lasciviousness.

"Our lips join in one long, long kiss. Our tongues stick together. Then I halt to gaze upon the beauties lower down. — Ah! God! — Sisters!" he cries, halting in his narrative, "Have mercy! Permit me to finish this story with stiffened tool."

"I cannot help myself, Father," returns Lucia.

"Nor yet can I," adds Robina. "Your fingering excites me so greatly that I lose command of myself."

"You break in upon his narrative," cries the Mother Abbess. "Contain yourselves, Sisters. Let us have no more interruption."

"Where was I?" asks Pedro, bewildered.

"You were just about to gaze upon the beauties lower down!" cry Ambrose, Joachim and Tasso in one voice.

A shout of laughter greets this involuntarily concerted answer.

"Ah! Yes!" resumed Pedro. "I gazed at the sight before me like a famished wolf. The white stomach, the magnificent thighs which were opening and shutting in gleeful anticipation, but best of all the mount of

Venus, the door of Paradise, the sweet silken-lined cunt. Between its moist and reddened lips nestled a half-blown rose, a symbol of virginity that Princesses of Spain have worn from the beginning of their history. None but a true virgin dare place a bud in such a receptacle.

"I uttered a shriek of delight at this most enchanting sight, removed the bud, and alternately kissed and sucked the unfucked slit. Then I played with the hxquisite clitoris until the couch groaned with her motions and tossings.

"My prick was now swollen to an enormous extent. As I glanced at it, I heard a voice say:

" 'The King's Stallion cannot compare with it.'

"It was the maid on the left who spoke. It was then that I became aware that the two whom I first saw upon my entrance, were still in attendance.

" 'Ah! My mistress will be split apart by such a monster!'

" 'Have no fear!' retorts the other. 'She will conquer it shortly, and reduce it to nothingness.'

"The Princess meanwhile was mad with passion. She pulls me vigorously towards her. I mount her, like the stallion that I am. My staff is burning with desire. I push open the tightly closed lips of the royal slit. Not a protest comes from her. Now I am in. I rage like a bull. I push. I snort. She bids me onward. I fuck and fuck. She foams at the mouth. I fuck and fuck more swiftly than before. My feet are on the floor. I am in a glorious position between her thighs. She then raises her feet, and places them upon my shoulders. Still I fuck and fuck until my balls are all but in the breach. Then I pause for breath.

"A loud shriek, expressive of overflowing joys, comes from her. Then I pounce upon her mouth and suck the sweetness from her lips.

"Thus glued together, I unloosed the long pent-up savings of my loins, and pour them into her inmost depths, so much so as to copiously drench every portion of her womb. Yet I did not withdraw myself. She seeks to throw me off. In vain! I fuck and fuck, she wildly gesticulating with her arms, and pressing me close with her dainty feet.

" Thus we lay, — how long I know not, nor cared. If I could have stayed thus, never would I have removed myself; but as such things must have an end, so it came in my case, too.

" ' Ha ! ' cries one of the maids. ' Did I not speak truth? See ! She has conquered it completely.'

" The Princess was lying in sweet confusion upon the couch. Her attendants did her needed service, and later, I too, was treated like a royal prince. Ere that night of pleasure had ended, I had fucked both the virgin maids of honor, each in turn, straight before the royal face.

" ' As these faithful maids have honored me, so I will honor them ! ' cries the Princess. 'Father ! ' she added, 'See ! They await your pleasure!'

" By the ten thousand virgins ! " swore Pedro. " How I did fuck them ! And their sobs of joy linger in my ears even yet ! And for a finale, the Princess with her dainty mouth sucked my hard-worked prick into an erect state, and in return I gave her such a bouncing as to completely drive all sickness entirely from her.

"Need I say more? Save that the Prince of Parma espoused the Princess of Spain a month later, and my master complimented me highly for the assistance I had lent in the affair. Some of the details in a mysterious manner became known in Church channels. Hence the title given me."

That Father Pedro's story was highly appreciated needs scarce to be mentioned. All present were infatuated with the tale. The orgies recommenced with renewed vigor, and the apartment witnessed scenes in which unbridled lust figured to an extent unimaginable even to the most depraved of human beings.

Aminda could be seen handling Tasso's fine prick with such vigorous jerks that it seemed as if she would dissever it from his body. He in turn was sucking her burning slit. He imprints long and hot kisses upon it. He implores her to have mercy upon his instrument of pleasure.

"Give me your cunt to fuck!" he begs.

She answers by throwing herself upon his tool, and fucks him with such gusto that he writhes about like a serpent.

Father Pedro has secured a stout birch, and commences to give the Mother Abbess' large fat arse a sound drubbing.

Lucia, Robina and Pampinea are chasing the naked priests Joachim and Ambrose around the apartment. Soon the five forms are intermingled. Cunts and pricks are fondled with eager touches. The prick of Ambrose enters Lucia's cunt. Joachim fucks Pampinea, while Robina enjoys the pleasure of having her cunt sucked in turn by the two priests.

Pedro is once more in superb shape. His large prick inflames the Mother Abbess to passions beyond control. She sucks it until it dwindles to flabbiness, and so the company enjoyed themselves until the faint beams of the rising sun bade them to disperse.

CHAPTER X.

ROSA WINDS IT UP

T HE lascivious pleasures which were so greatly enjoyed by all who were present at the amorous orgie just described in our last chapter, were unfortunately never repeated; for, a few days later Fathers Joachim, Pedro and Ambrose received summons from those high in authority, commanding their presence elsewhere.

The Mother Abbess and the Sisters were deeply grieved when the Fathers informed them of this fact.

"Alas!" cried the Mother Abbess, as she affectionately embraced in turn each of these departing priests. "Who shall now give our hungry cunts solace? It was only this very morning that our Tasso left for a month's absence. His aged parent is in a decline, and needs his son's presence to cheer his dying hours."

"Ah!" sighed the beautiful Robina. "What ill fortune is ours!"

"Restrain your grief," said Father Pedro, mournfully, "or you will but add to our own."

The three Fathers then and there fucked the Mother Abbess and the four Sisters until the entire party were deluged with blissful feelings. They fucked and sucked until exhaustion forced them all to halt.

After the departure of the lusty monks, affairs in the Convent resumed their usual state. Two attenuated, wrinkled Friars now acted the part of Confessors. They were lean and shrivelled, and in strong contrast to the strong and sturdy monks whom they had succeeded.

The Mother Abbess was loud in her complaints.

"How dare they inflict such scarecrows upon us?" she protested, indignantly, to the Sisters.

"Their stinking breaths show that their

stomachs are starved with improper food," interjected Lucia.

"And one of them," spoke up Aminda, "bade me to sacrifice my appetite and not indulge it so freely."

"The dastards!" exclaimed the Mother Abbess. "They would have our stomachs as foul as their own. I am of the opinion that their shrunken tools would not secure an erection, even if we were to attempt the disgusting task of trying."

"Horrid thought!" said Lucia, laughing. "No doubt," she added, "but they are so virtuous that they fail to pay attention to the calls of nature."

"Then say I," rejoins the Mother Abbess, "may they foul themselves to perdition with their own urine."

Sad indeed were the straits in which the unfortunate band of Sisters now found themselves.

"'Tis more than we can bear," said Aminda to the Mother Abbess some time afterwards. "Pampinea and myself are determined to leave this life. We shall go out into the world, find proper husbands, and be fucked every night."

"Oh! Will not that be truly delightful?"
returned the Mother Abbess.

Shortly afterwards they carried out their
determination and both were fortunate enough
to secure lusty gallants as husbands, who, no
doubt to their great satisfaction, plowed
them well.

The Mother Abbess, with Lucia and
Robina were now forced to seek gratification
in each other's company. They often fucked
one another in the feminine manner, with
tongue and finger, and thus to some extent
made up for the loss of the Fathers and
Tasso.

About this time, an addition was made to
their company in the shape of a beautiful
young girl, Rosa by name. She had sought
the Convent to escape the machinations of
those related to her. A deceased uncle had
left her a snug fortune, the possession of
which had excited the envy of those closely
allied to her. To free herself from their
persecutions, she had fled to the Convent.

Lucia and Robina were soon on intimate
terms with her.

"She is truly a virgin," said Lucia to her
companion. "It was but yesterday that I

asked her if she knew what prick meant. —
She immediately answered in the negative.

" 'Prick is what men possess,' I explained,
'It is soft at first, but when a woman touches
it, the thing grows large and stiff.'

" 'Oh! Yes!' she responded. 'I know
now. You mean that which a man pees with.
I did not quite understand at first.'

"I asked her if she knew what a cunt was,
and she replied in the negative as before.
When I told her, she blushed scarlet. I then
spoke of the great pleasure to be obtained by
joining prick with cunt, and then I further
said,

" 'If you will let me, I will play with your
cunt to give you some conception of what
would happen when a man lies in bed with
you.' And Oh!" continued Lucia, hotly,
"would you believe it? She permitted me to
play with her cunt for a long time. It made
me sick with pleasure, and I told her to play
with my slit as I did with hers; and soon our
arses were bounding away in a manner that
would set a man crazy to behold."

"I must play with her too," interrupted
Robina, in an eager tone.

"Oh! She is so fresh and sweet!" returned

Lucia, "that I would love to see her fucked for the first time!"

"Happy thought!" cried Robina. "You know Tasso returns to-morrow. Would it not be an excellent idea to have him fuck her? A month's absence must have given him renewed strength."

"I will make mention of it to him," replied Lucia.

The next day when Tasso returned, Lucia brought Sister Rosa to him as he was working in the garden with the old gardener. Tasso saw the signal and went at once to her.

The novice was much pleased with the appearance of the gardener; and when Robina and Lucia had told her what he had done to them, she too seemed desirous of testing his ability to please.

"We are all nearly starved," said Robina to Rosa. "Our cunts are just watering for a man; but we will restrain ourselves in order that you may enjoy the bliss of being fucked. It will also be a source of great pleasure to the Mother Abbess if you will permit her to see you fucked by Tasso."

Now Rosa was as tempting a piece of woman-flesh as the eye of mortal man ever beheld. She was short and plump in figure, with a lovely face, expressive of a mirthful disposition. Her blue eyes were large and lustrous; and there was that in them which would make any healthy man's prick rise very quickly. The lily and the rose fought for supremacy in her cheeks, and the luscious red mouth was one to gloat over, to sigh for, to dream about.

Tasso fell head over heels in love with Rosa at first sight, and when Lucia told him of the feast she had in store for him, he knelt at her feet in worship. He raised her robe and kissed her tempting slit, whilst she in turn played with his fine prick.

"We have determined to deny ourselves," she said, removing herself from him. "You must save yourself for Rosa."

The following evening the Mother Abbess, in company with Lucia, Robina and Rosa, assembled in the apartment which had been the scene of their former orgie. Tasso did not keep them waiting; for hardly had the four entered than he made his appearance.

The blushing Rosa was at first quite backward, but the hot-blooded Tasso soon cured her bashfulness; for he pressed her tempting bosom and played with her tight little cunt until she was in a high state of sexual excitement,

The Mother Abbess and the two Sisters will now describe the exciting contest.

"See! Tasso is quite naked!" says Robina. "How large his prick looks! — Oh! Rosa! How your backside will jump up and down when his thing is in you!"

"Rosa is bashful! She still has her gown on. — There! That is right, Tasso! Take it off and fuck her naked!"

"Look at her swelling slit! — Is it not lovely?" observes the Mother Abbess." "Tasso likes it! — See him kiss it! — That's right, Rosa. Move your arse about! — There! Lay down upon the couch! Tasso will now work your clitoris until you spend."

"Oh! This is a feast!" interjects Tasso, as he sucks Rosa's mouth, and rubs her cunt in a vigorous manner.

"Play with his balls, Rosa! — Yes! In that manner! For it will make his prick stiffer," advises Robina.

"They are both getting in shape for a good fuck!" she continues. "Look, Mother! Rosa has commenced to spend."

"Play with my cunt, both of you!" entreats the Mother Abbess, who was now in a high state of excitement.

"Tasso, do not tease her so! Her cunt is eager for your prick!" expostulated Lucia. "That is proper," she continues. "See, Robina! His prick is going in, and Rosa is pushing her arse forward! — She wants it so badly."

"How closely her cunt clings to his prick!" said Robina, who was watching the two with eager eyes.

"Oh! God! — This is pleasure, indeed!" shouts Tasso. "Her cunt is like a vice! — Oh! Ah! Ah! My balls will burst with bliss!"

"Now fuck her, Tasso! Fuck her!" almost shrieks the Mother Abbess. "Your big prick has opened her fresh cunt for the first time! — That is why it is so tight."

"His prick is all wet!" says Robina. "She must be spending."

"Ah! My finger is all wet also," cries Lucia. "Mother, you too have come off!"

"Oh! Do but see him!" admiringly exclaims the Mother Abbess. "Ah! That thrust touched her to the very quick!"

And indeed, so it seemed, for the beautiful Rosa became wild with bliss; and when Tasso halted a moment, she twisted herself on top of him and fucked and fucked him until she had drained him entirely.

When he removed his prick the three waiting women took possession of it; and when they were through, poor Tasso was as weak as a cat.

The day following, Rosa, in company with Tasso, fled from the Convent. Tasso feared that he would fade away into a veritable shadow if he continued to dwell amongst such amorous women.

Tasso and Rosa were married without delay, and continued faithful to one another for the remainder of their lives. A large family of children blessed them.

A few weeks after the flight of Tasso, Robina and Lucia followed his example, and were espoused later by two noble gentlemen, who frequently wondered at their wives' marvellous knowledge of the art of fucking. Of course the modest girls always kept them in a complete state of ignorance respecting the school in which they were so ably taught.

The Mother Abbess one day horrified her Confessor with a vulgar remark. The poor woman had been deprived of sexual food so long that she was scarcely conscious of her words.

She saluted him with the following:

"Scarecrow! Your stinking breath would shame a shit-house!"

The horrified priest at once reported this remark to his Superiors, but before the resultant penalty had time to be announced to the Mother Abbess, she had gathered up her belongings, and returned, like a sensible woman, to the world. As she was possessed of large means, and thus being able to gratify her desires, she hired ponderous footmen; and when they were fucked out, she would present them with a handsome stipend, and replace them with others more sturdy. She maintained this state for long years, occasionally varying her diet with a good fat oily friar, until finally her dwelling-place became known to the curious as a "place where fat men got thin," or, in modern parlance, an anti-fat cure. But, as death comes to all, so in due time he came to the Mother Abbess. Her place of burial is celebrated to this day in consequence of the curious monument that ornaments her last resting place. It is an immense stone, partly rounded, and a very close imitation of a stiff prick. Thus can be seen, even the ruling passion strong in death.

EXTRACT FROM THE MINUTES.

At a stated meeting of the *Societé des Beaux Esprits* held on the 15th November 1897, the following report was submitted.

Your committee on Antiquarian Research, in submitting its report desires to call the attention of the members of the Society once more to the bequest of the late M. Jerome, a former member.

M. Jerome made a most generous bequest to us in 1896 of a large sum of money to be expended, as his will read "in the investigation of doubtful claims of authors who presume to wear borrowed plumes and thus filch the brain-work of honest though less known writers, with particular reference to authors and works named in a memorandum placed in the hands of the Secretary of the aforesaid Society."

Your committee desires to state that in pursuance of these duties, it has made a careful search not only through the libraries of the Louvre in Paris, but also the public and private libraries of London, Berlin, Florence,

Rome, Milan, and divers other places, as well as our beloved city Bruxelles; and after with due care weighing the arguments for and against, we have arrived at the conclusion that the celebrated tale, Novel 1, of the third day of the *Decameron*, (familiarly known as "Massetto and the Nuns,") written by a certain Giovanni Boccaccio, and likewise several weaker imitations, owe their origin to the present work which we now lay before you, entitled *Lascivious Scenes in the Convent.* Our sub-committee has carefully and freely translated this work from the original Tuscan, into English and French, modernising it to such an extent that persons even of mean capacity may read it understandingly.

All of which is respectfully submitted.

THE COMMITTEE.

The report having been adopted, it was unanimously decided to place it upon the minutes of the Society, and the Committee was thereupon discharged from further action.